W9-AVW-449

Shine Mountain

Shine Mountain

Julie Hunt

ALLEN&UNWIN
SYDNEY · MELBOURNE · AUCKLAND · LONDON

First published by Allen & Unwin in 2018

Copyright © Julie Hunt 2018

All rights reserved. No part of this book may be reproduced
or transmitted in any form or by any means, electronic or mechanical,
including photocopying, recording or by any information storage
and retrieval system, without prior permission in writing from the
publisher. The *Australian Copyright Act 1968* (the Act) allows a
maximum of one chapter or ten per cent of this book, whichever is
the greater, to be photocopied by any educational institution for its
educational purposes provided that the educational institution
(or body that administers it) has given a remuneration notice
to Copyright Agency Limited (CAL) under the Act.

Allen & Unwin
83 Alexander Street
Crows Nest NSW 2065
Australia
Phone: (61 2) 8425 0100
Email: info@allenandunwin.com
Web: www.allenandunwin.com

A catalogue record for this
book is available from the
National Library of Australia

ISBN 978 1 76029 150 1

For teaching resources, explore
www.allenandunwin.com/resources/for-teachers

Cover and text design by Ruth Grüner
Cover illustrations by Geoff Kelly, Ruth Grüner, FCIT
Map by Geoff Kelly
Set in 12.2 pt Granjon by Ruth Grüner

Printed in Australia in March 2018 by McPherson's Printing Group

1 3 5 7 9 10 8 6 4 2

MIX
Paper from
responsible sources
FSC® C001695
www.fsc.org

The paper in this book is FSC certified.
FSC promotes environmentally responsible,
socially beneficial and economically viable
management of the world's forests.

FOR SUE FLOCKHART

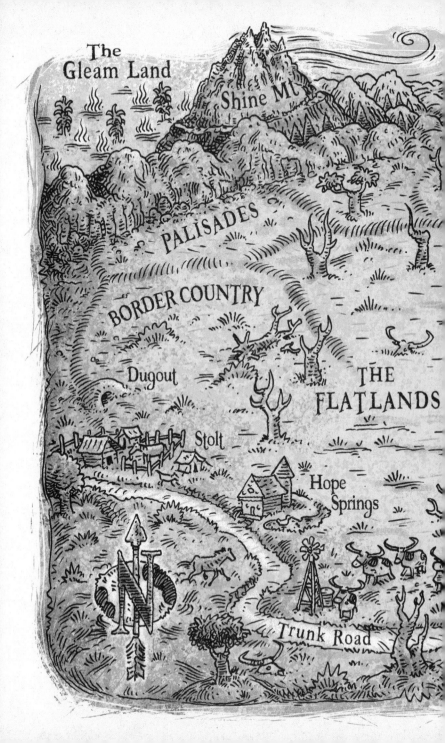

PART ONE

1

Spit Farm

'ELLIE, STOP YOUR MOOCHING and bring the rest of Pop's things.' Oma bustled past me, carrying my grandfather's big sheepskin coat. 'Meet you at the washpool,' she said.

I was watching the weather turn and the snow blow in across the mountains, but I swung myself onto the verandah and clomped inside the shack. The place was crowded with cousins and their boxes and bags. They'd come from the towns on the plains and they'd brought enough supplies to last all winter, saying they didn't know how long it was going to take.

'It' meant Pop's death, I knew. I hated it when they said that. Pop was failing, and he looked smaller every day, but he could still talk and sing, and so far there'd been no sign of the shine-moth, which made me hope he wouldn't die at all.

I grabbed Pop's shirt and the socks from his boots

and headed down the path that led to the washpool.
I could see the goats moving below amid clouds of
steam. The ground near the pool was warm from the
water and they grazed there because the snow melted
as fast as it fell. As I approached, the lead doe, Nanny
Gitto, lifted her head. She was my favourite and Oma's
too. She gave me a long, steady look as if to say, 'Don't
worry, Ellie, it'll work out.'

'What'll work out?' I asked. When I was little I used
to imagine Nanny talked, giving me advice and answering all my questions. 'Will they all go away? Will Pop
come good?'

'None of that,' Oma said. 'No nattering. Let's get the
washing done.'

She was stripped to the waist and sudding up, both
herself and Pop's coat, and the warm water frothed
around her. Her basket sat on the bank.

'Into the churn.'

She pointed to a slatted tub she had tied under the
chute and I shoved Pop's things under the hot running
water.

'Not the socks,' she yelled. 'They'll felt.'

I reached in and got them out, almost scalding
myself in the process. Oma waded towards me through
the steam. She took the socks and gently squeezed them
out. Muddy water dripped down her arms.

'I knitted these,' she muttered, holding them against
her cheek. 'Only a couple of winters ago.'

'He mightn't die, Oma,' I said. 'People get well
again, don't they?'

My grandmother shook her head. 'He has to die now, what with them all here and waiting.' She gave a sad sort of chuckle, then she wrung out the socks and slapped them over the railing alongside Auntie Lil's singlets.

'I don't care for a party,' I told her.

'It's what Pop wants. No one leaves without a good send-off. We'll dance all night.'

'I won't.'

Oma took my hand. 'In your mind, my dear, if not on the ground.'

'I won't dance anywhere.'

Oma sighed.

'You're a stubborn girl, Ellie West.'

She took a carding comb from her basket and handed it to me.

'Brush my hair, girl. Brush it all away.'

That's what she always said. She meant her troubles, and I was one of them.

I undid Oma's plaits and brushed out her silver hair, sweeping it over her shoulder so that it flowed down her back like a waterfall. Having her hair brushed was Oma's favourite thing. She lifted her face to the sky and a snowflake landed on her cheek.

'Look at Ossa,' she said. 'The pass will be closed soon.'

Mt Ossa towered above us. I could just see it through the clouds. Already the top of it was capped up white as a tooth and an icy wind blew up from the valley.

'Pop will go before the pass closes,' I said.

Oma looked at me closely. 'Really? Did you get one of your feelings?'

I nodded and she looked over my shoulder, frowning towards the pass.

'I wish the lawyer would come,' she said.

Pop had sent for a lawyer. He wanted to make a will and get everything written down in front of a stranger so there'd be no arguments. That's what he said. I didn't see what there was to argue over. Oma would get the farm and the animals. My brother Tod would get Sol, Pop's horse. Maybe there were a few leftover things, like Pop's grandmother's moonstone necklace that had hung over the fireplace for as long as I could remember, or his banjo, or the old suit he'd worn when he went to the plains long ago.

I ran my fingers through Oma's hair. It was long and thick, like mine. I liked to think we were two of a kind, but thick hair was the only thing we shared. I didn't look like any of my family and on bad days my Auntie Shirl swore I was a ring-in.

'That'll do, El.' My grandmother took the comb from my hand. 'Let's be getting back.'

Pop's coat was too heavy to carry up the hill so we left it dripping on the railing. With a bit of luck it wouldn't freeze overnight.

Sol was waiting outside the shack when we came up the path. He stood with his head down and his back to the wind. Tod was leaning against him, his hair blowing about his face.

My brother was thirteen, a year older than me, but he was small and seemed younger. He stroked Sol's flank and said, 'How will he be when Pop's gone?' But he was talking about himself, not Sol.

Tod was closer to Pop than anyone. He scowled across the yard at a group of relatives who were sitting outside the holdfast. It was usually full of animal feed and supplies for winter but now it was full of people.

'Why are they here, Oma?' he asked. 'Pop doesn't even know half of them.'

I wondered that too. It seemed a long way to come for a party, although Oma and Pop always said the shindigs held on the flatlands were nothing compared with those in the mountains.

When Oma didn't answer, Tod buried his face in Sol's neck.

'Feed him, Tod, then go and tend the ponies,' Oma said. 'Ellie, go and see your grandfather.'

I went inside to the front room. The shack was full to bursting and wherever there was a spare bit of floor someone had a bedroll on it.

Pop was talking to one of the town uncles, a big man called Wade, who I liked more than the others. He carried a hammer in his belt and he'd fixed the yard gate on the day he arrived, then made himself a lean-to beside the shed, using old boards we'd had lying about. After that he felled a tree and milled it. Tod and I had watched as he planed the wood, the slivers peeling off in long golden curls and the air filled with the scent of musk pine. He made a burial box for Pop out of those sweet-smelling planks and my grandfather was happy to see it so well crafted.

I got the sense that Wade had come just to help and pay his respects. With the others, I wasn't so sure.

Pop was laughing at something Wade said, but his laughter ended in a coughing fit. He struggled for breath for a moment before sitting up and smiling at me.

'Here's the girl,' he said.

'You're feeling better, Pop. I can tell.'

'Sometimes the fire shines brightest just before it goes out.' He gave me a wink and then he pointed to the window. 'Call the goats.'

I opened it and leaned out, yelling, '*Yidda yidda yidda!*'

Some relatives, standing outside, turned in surprise and when I looked over my shoulder, Pop's eyes were twinkling.

'Powerful, ain't she?' he said to Wade. 'They can hear her all the way to the Palisades.'

He reached out his hand and I held it. 'Look after Oma for me,' he said, suddenly serious. 'Promise me.'

'Of course, Pop.' Tears pricked my eyes.

'And Tod as well. We look after our own in this family. You've got to stick together.' He squeezed my hand. 'Now go and help your Oma. They'll be putting on the feedbag soon.'

I left Pop and went out the front to where Oma, Lil and Auntie Shirl were busy with the cooking. The goats were already halfway up the hill. I could hear them coming, the does calling their kids and the kids bleating in reply.

'If I've told you once I've told you a hundred times, Ellie – don't bring them this way,' Shirl muttered. 'It's muddy enough as it is.'

Most of the cousins were gathered around the firepit and when Nanny Gitto led the goats through, the crowd parted, half of them stepping up on the verandah and the others backing towards the holdfast. They glanced at each other as Nanny passed, pausing to sniff a cooking pot that sat on the ground by the fire.

There were three children among the cousins and one of them was a girl my age. She followed me into the barn with the goats, staring at my boot. Then she stood with her arms folded as I mixed up the mash and put it in the feeding trough. The six goats we were milking went into their stalls.

'What happened to your foot?' she asked. 'Did you break it or were you born with it?'

'Born,' I muttered. I don't like people talking about my foot.

'Do your parents have odd feet? Is it something that's passed down?'

'Course not,' I replied, although I didn't really know because my pa had left before I was born and my mother died when I was a baby.

'You know what my pa said?' she whispered. 'He said a foot like that's a gift. No one can follow your tracks in the snow and if they do, they can't work out if you're going forwards or backwards.' She burst out laughing.

I put my hands on my hips. 'Why are you all here?'
I demanded.

She shrugged. 'Ma said we were invited.'

She turned her attention to Nanny Gitto. 'You have
weird animals. I've never seen a goat like that before.'

Nanny was tall. She had long spiral horns and a
white coat that almost reached the ground. We only had
one goat like her but I told the girl we had a whole herd
of them hidden in the back country west of Mt Ossa.

'They're very valuable. Their milk makes you wise
and the curd made from that milk can cure any illness.'

'That's mountain talk. I don't believe it,' the girl
said. 'If that was true you wouldn't have a crooked foot.'

I ignored her. 'Their horns grow one spiral every ten
years and that's how you can tell their age. And they can
understand human language.'

She gave me a scornful look. 'If you believe that, you
believe anything.'

'The soap made from their milk is so strong it can
lift the stains off your character,' I told her.

I picked up a bucket and began milking Nanny.

When the girl came close and looked over my
shoulder I whispered, 'This goat comes from the Gleam
country.'

'There's no such place,' she replied. 'You're telling
lies.'

'There is and I know all about it.'

'How could you? You haven't been anywhere.'

That was true. I'd never even been to the Trading
Post. I'd lived all my life on Spit Farm but I knew my

own mountain like the back of my hand. I knew all the
tracks and trails and sometimes when I closed my eyes
I could see tunnels running under the ground as well, a
network that led from Mt Ossa to the rest of the world.
I called them the underways and they were as real to me
as the trails above the ground.

'The corn in the Gleam country grows so big the
people have to fell it with an axe.'

'That's enough, Ellie.'

Oma came into the barn. She reached for a bucket
and squatted beside the first goat in the row. 'Your ma
wants you,' she told the girl, and when the cousin left
she turned to me.

'Behave yourself. They're guests.'

'I wasn't doing anything, just telling her about
Nanny.'

Oma frowned into her bucket and began squirting
the milk.

'Don't talk moonshine, Ellie. You're a big girl now
and with Pop going I need you to be strong, not carrying
on like a three-year-old. I need you to grow up. Will you
do that for me?'

'All right,' I said, although I didn't know if it was
possible.

2

The Shine-moth

SOL WASN'T LIKE our other horses. They were grey mountain ponies but Sol was broad and black and shining as if he'd been polished. He had a white mark on his shoulder in the shape of a crescent moon and you could see it at night when the rest of him disappeared in darkness. Pop believed Sol had come to us in the old days before the family broke up and went their separate ways. There used to be a big settlement here – you could still see the stump holes where the huts had stood. Sol was left over from that time, along with a few other things that weren't so special: a couple of old ploughs that were rotting into the ground, the stone water trough near the back door and a few odds and ends that Pop kept in a crate under his bed.

I sat on the fence stroking Sol's soft nose and looking at the cousins who milled around the shack waiting for dinner. There must have been twenty or more, and they were just the ones I could see.

'It's all right, Sol. They'll leave soon,' I said, and he put his nose to my face to show me he agreed. He flicked his ears when Auntie Lil banged the dinner gong. She called me over to help.

'Don't be heavy handed,' she said, as she gave me the ladle. 'Our supplies won't last forever.'

I helped her serve the meal but I didn't eat myself. I wasn't hungry. While everyone else was having dinner I sat on the end of the verandah, podding the last of the season's tick beans. Oma came and sat beside me.

'No sorrows, El,' she said.

She squeezed my hand and looked towards the pass. 'See him yet? Your eyes are younger than mine.'

There was nobody coming. Oma took the beans and went inside.

My uncle Vern was sitting on a stump next to the firepit talking to some cousins and I went and sat near him.

'There's drought out west,' a fellow wrapped in a blanket was saying. 'You're lucky to live in the mountains.'

Vern sucked on his pipe and nodded. He was looking into the coals and the lantern on the verandah lit one side of his weathered face.

There were strains of music coming from the holdfast, a fiddle tuning up and someone twanging on a jaw harp. Some of the cousins stood up and headed in that direction.

'They should wait,' I said.

'I don't know. Your pop wouldn't mind. Why don't you join the dancing?'

He smiled and raised one eyebrow.

I liked Uncle Vern. He was Pop's brother. He knew I didn't dance. He was one of the few people who'd seen my foot. He looked at it every year so he could measure me up for boots. He made all our boots and it was just as well because the ones at the Trading Post cost a fortune.

'It's a pity Ort can't join in,' he said as he drew on his pipe.

'Maybe he could,' I suggested. 'We could take him over.'

'His dancing days are done, girl.'

I leaned close to my uncle. The night was cold and there was hardly anyone left by the fire. 'Why are all these cousins here?' I asked.

'Some family business,' he replied vaguely. 'I expect the lawyer will sort it out.'

'Where's he coming from?' the man with the blanket asked.

'Scarp,' Uncle Vern replied. 'But I can't see him getting over the pass in this weather.'

'Why's the lawyer coming, Uncle?' I whispered. 'Pop's not rich or anything.'

He blew a cloud of smoke into the air and watched it disappear.

'Time for me to turn in. Goodnight, Ellie.'

I watched him walk away, his boots making a sucking sound in the mud, then I went inside the shack.

In the back room, Oma was in bed. She wasn't asleep, though – I could tell by her breathing.

'Any sign of him?' she asked.

I told her there wasn't.

'What about the shine-moth?'

'No sign of that either.'

She gave a sigh. When I got in beside her she put an arm around me and fell asleep.

THE SHINE-MOTH ARRIVED that night. I heard the thrum of its wings through the wooden walls of the shack. It was so loud it made the roof stones rattle. I sat bolt upright and stared into the dark, surprised that nobody else could hear it. Auntie Lil had come to bed and was snoring on the other side of Oma, and there was no movement from the cousins who were asleep on the floor.

'Oma,' I whispered. 'It's come.'

She rubbed her eyes. 'Go and look,' she murmured. 'But don't frighten it.'

As soon as I opened the back door the noise stopped. The night was clear and cold and the wind chilled my nose and fingertips. The moon was halfway across the sky and the stars were bright, but apart from that, nothing shone. Then I saw a flicker in the corner of my eye. The moth was perched on the door frame and it was no bigger than a horsefly. It brushed my cheek as it flew into the shack, a tiny spark disappearing into the front room. I followed, carefully sidestepping the people on the floor. A slab of moonlight fell on Pop's bed and I saw the shine-moth land on the bedhead. It was still for a moment, then it opened its wings and began a slow, steady beating. Pop gave a sigh as the insect took over his breathing. He looked so relieved I thought he might die right then, and I was about to get Oma when he turned and opened his eyes.

'Tod all right?' he asked.

I nodded and took Pop's hand. I wanted to tell him that he didn't have to die just because the lawyer was coming.

He squeezed my fingers and said, 'I'm old as the hills, El. My time has come.'

The shine-moth flared slightly then settled into a soft pulsing glow. It seemed to be getting brighter with each wing beat. When the dogs outside began barking it paused for a second, then continued. I heard the front door open.

'He's here!' someone yelled.

People stirred and I heard Oma putting on the kettle. 'He'll need a bed,' she said.

I left Pop and went outside. The lawyer dismounted his horse in front of the verandah, panting in the thin mountain air. He was a brittle-looking fellow with a sharp face that shone in the moonlight and he didn't look impressed with Spit Farm. Maybe he expected some grand place instead of our flimsy shack and the scattering of outbuildings. He took in the mud and snow, the shaggy ponies and the motley collection of people who were quickly gathering around him, and shook his head as if he couldn't believe it.

Oma took the man's oilskin coat.

'You must be tired,' she said. 'Come inside and I'll fix you some breakfast, then you can rest.'

The man looked down his nose at my grandmother. She was wearing her woolly jacket over her nightgown. Perhaps he expected her to be properly dressed.

'I'd prefer to start immediately,' he said.

Oma led him into the shack. I followed right behind and so did everyone else who could fit. The city cousins pushed their way in. They pressed themselves against the wall, trying to keep as far away from the shine-moth as possible, as if they thought it was carrying something they might catch. I could have told them there was nothing to fear. The moth was only doing its job, the same as a borer or a bloat worm or a buzzard – it didn't come to kill a person, it came to help their passing. And it never came uninvited – that's what Oma said. But our relatives were superstitious. One of the women stared at the bedhead with narrow eyes and grasped her hands tightly. You could see she wanted to swat it.

Oma fixed the pillows behind Pop. She gave the lawyer a box to sit on next to the bed. From his satchel he took out a wad of papers, a small bottle of ink, a pen and a pair of spectacles. Then he called for a writing table. Uncle Vern went out the back and levered a plank off the porch. He brought it inside, resting one end on the bed and holding the other.

The lawyer put his papers on it and the crowd leaned

forward, eager and waiting. Oma was the only one who looked calm. It was as if she already knew what was about to happen.

'What's your name, son?' Pop asked the lawyer.

The fellow wasn't young but I guess he was young to Pop.

'Alexis,' he replied. 'Alexis Strand.'

The top of the page was half full of writing and the lawyer began filling in the gaps.

'This is the Last Will and Testament of...' He wrote down Pop's name in small spidery letters: Orton West. There was no sound in the room except for the scratching of his pen.

'I hereby revoke all Former Wills—'

'There's none,' Oma said.

Alexis Strand began making a list of everything on Spit Farm: the land, the timber, the tools, the holdfast, the chook house, the sheds and the shack. It was still dark when he had started on the livestock: forty goats including six milkers, a house cow and two heifers, a dozen fat-tailed sheep, one trail ox, some mixed-breed mountain ponies, one black gelding of unknown origin, two sows and a porker... the list went on.

I suddenly remembered Pop's coat hanging on the railing and I whispered in Oma's ear.

'Go and get it,' she said. 'Take Tod with you.'

My brother was sitting near Pop's head watching the shine-moth. When I took his hand he leaned close. 'It's growing bigger, El. It's nearly the size of a butterfly.'

We pushed our way out the door and a couple more

people slipped inside to take our place. The girl who'd come into the barn was on the verandah.

'Where are you going?' she asked, as I took a lantern from the hook. She followed us down to the wash and I was glad of that because it took the three of us to carry Pop's damp coat. By the time we got back the lawyer had finished the will and was reading it out. We hung the coat in the porch and squeezed in the doorway to listen.

The moonstone necklace went to Auntie Lil. Wade got Pop's banjo and some of the tools – an adze, two crosscut saws and a hatchet. Oma got the farm and the livestock. Tod got Sol. I got Nanny Gitto. It was all exactly as expected.

'"And, in addition to the farm, I leave a song, which I will play on the instrument that is to be buried with me,"' the lawyer read.

Everyone was suddenly alert. Pop motioned for Tod to get something from the crate under the bed. I thought it was a little jewel box at first. It was a pretty thing with a pattern of leaves carved on what seemed to be the lid, but when Tod opened it I realised it was a button-box, a tiny concertina.

I was surprised by the reaction it caused. A murmur ran through the relatives at the sight of it.

'Buried with him? A waste!' someone muttered.

Alexis Strand stroked his chin and stared at the instrument. I stared too. It was old. The bellows were cracked and patched and some of the buttons were broken. It looked as if it had been in a fire. There was a burn mark on one end.

Pop asked for people to move away from the window. It was almost dawn outside and I could see the shape of Ossa against the sky. Pop stared at the mountain then he told Oma to stand at the end of the bed.

'Remember when we were young, Flo?' he said, as he took the tiny instrument in his hands. A few silverfish fell onto the blanket. He extended the bellows and when he squeezed them shut there was no note at first, just a soft hissing sound. A musty smell filled the room and the shine-moth lost its rhythm. It fluttered wildly for a moment before landing on Pop's shoulder, where it resumed the steady fanning of its wings.

Pop started to play and, to my surprise, the thing made a good sound, sweet and mellow. My grandfather began to sing. He didn't have much strength but he sang about springtime in the mountains. It wasn't a song I'd heard but Oma seemed to know it and she joined in with a harmony. Soon the cousins were singing too, and our little shack was full of a sound that seemed almost too big for it. Some of the goats started bleating from the barn and one of the dogs howled.

The lawyer grew agitated as the song went on. He wanted to get the will signed and witnessed so he could go.

Oma was gazing at Pop and singing at the top of her voice. She was framed in the window against Mt Ossa. Maybe it was the light behind her that made her look strange. Her silver hair seemed dark and shiny and there was a rosy flush on her cheeks. She looked like a young woman. Her eyes gleamed and tears stood in them.

Oma rarely cried but when she did I always cried as well. It was something I couldn't stop. My eyes filled and then I couldn't see clearly. I wiped my face on Pop's bedclothes and looked again. Oma was herself once more and nobody else seemed to have noticed.

The shine-moth increased the speed of its wingbeats and Pop's voice grew stronger. It wasn't a sad song; it was a song that made you feel like dancing and it had more verses to it than knots in a drag rope. The moon went behind a cloud and the room darkened. We all began to sway to the music, even the city cousins. The lawyer tapped his pen on the plank and called for order, but Pop kept playing. His eyes were blue as the sky and his skin took on a transparent look, like ice. He stared at Oma and his eyes widened. Mine did too. A vine was creeping across the glass behind her. I could see it clearly in the grey light outside. The mountain berry that grew under the window had long since died back for the winter but this new shoot was moving across the bottom pane. The tip of it branched and two fine tendrils spiralled upwards, looking for a hold. Some of the cousins stopped singing and one of the city aunts gave a little cry, clutching the person next to her.

Pop looked beyond the vine to the mountain, his wispy hair lifting a little, perhaps with the breath from the bellows, or maybe the breeze from the wings of the shine-moth. It was much larger now, like a small bat or a bird, and its wings were a silver blur.

Pop focused on Mt Ossa, which suddenly loomed taller than ever before. The first rays of the sun hit its peak just as the song ended. Pop smiled and squeezed the button-box shut, and the shine-moth closed its wings. The room grew very still. I heard the lawyer's pen roll off the plank onto the floor.

Auntie Lil put her hand to her face and gasped. I stared out the window. At first I thought the mountain was growing. The bare rock, the ironstone, was coming through the ice; it caught the morning sun and shone bright pink. Slowly I realised what was happening – the ice cap was melting. Then came the roar of rushing water as the ice on Mt Ossa dissolved into the myriad creeks that fed Spit River. We heard it crashing over the falls and into the valley below, a thundering echo that rang around the mountains.

Wade gave a long slow whistle and the cousins began to applaud, hesitantly at first and then with great gusto, whooping and cheering. I turned to Pop. He was still smiling and it seemed as though he was about to say something when Oma leaned over him. I thought she was going to whisper in his ear but instead she closed his eyes and, with a sigh, put her head on his chest.

The applause stopped and a shocked silence filled the room. People lowered their heads. Wade put his hand on Oma's shoulder and helped her to sit. The lawyer was brushed aside and Oma sat in his place on the box beside Pop's bed. She took a deep breath and looked at the papers on the plank.

'It's not signed,' she said. 'But it's done and we all witnessed it. Get the box, Wade.'

3

Nutt Rock

WE PUT POP'S COAT in the box. I was sorry that it was still wet but I guess it didn't matter. Wade and Uncle Vern laid Pop carefully on top of it with the button-box held over his chest. I put his boots next to his feet and we carried him outside and set the box on the verandah so Oma could decorate it. She used a dried sunflower as the centrepiece and surrounded it with springs of dogwood and spruce. It was the wrong time of year to go looking for wildflowers but some pippy-vine had sprouted by the back door – I'd seen it when I went to get Pop's coat – so I picked that and trailed the blue flowers over the lid. Oma tied goat bells on either end.

Everyone was outside. Some sat and stared at Mt Ossa; others, including Auntie Lil, examined the vine that had grown over the window.

'It's not the mountain berry,' she said. 'It's some sort of climber. It might be a kind of pumpkin, a moon melon perhaps. Fancy growing at this time of the year.'

Uncle Vern brought a barrel of cider from the holdfast and the lawyer helped himself to several cups.

'You'd better be on your way if you want to reach the way-hut by dark,' Oma told him.

The lawyer didn't leave. This puzzled me, because earlier he looked as though he didn't want to stay a moment longer than he had to. Now he stood at the end of Pop's box as if he was guarding it.

He stood there all morning. Uncle Vern went off and dug the grave and some of the cousins collected wood for the wake, a hard job at this time of the year. By the time they'd returned and built a bonfire the lawyer had found a chair and was sitting examining his papers, glancing from the will to Pop's box and back again as if he suspected some mistake. He rested his cup of cider on the lid until Oma told him to move it.

Auntie Lil and Shirl prepared a lunch of bread and cheese, then Oma put on a smock and told everyone to get ready. The relatives changed into their good clothes and Auntie Lil exchanged her work boots for a pair of flat shoes. I didn't have anything special to wear but Oma gave me some ribbons for my hair, one for each plait.

Tod saddled Sol then Uncle Vern and Wade and a couple of cousins shouldered Pop's box and we set off along the track past the yards, walking slowly. The cousins followed and the lawyer came along behind, leading his horse. Nanny Gitto never liked to miss out on things and she came too, the herd trailing after her.

The bells gave the procession a festive air but it wasn't as if we had anything to celebrate.

The air was warm and the ground was all mud and slush now, as most of the snow had melted. By the time we reached the yards I was sweating.

'It's unseasonable,' Wade said, wiping his brow. 'A hot spring day at the start of winter.'

It was mid-afternoon by the time we arrived at the grave. Uncle Vern had chosen a clearing in the pine forest near Jutt Rock.

'Is it deep enough?' Oma asked. 'We don't want him troubled by range-cats.'

'We should have brought the lamp,' Auntie Lil said. 'It'll be dark by the time we get back.'

She sent me to get it and when I reached the shack I stood for a moment in the doorway of Pop's room. It was empty but it felt like Pop was still there. His hat was hanging on the wall where he'd left it and it looked so lonely that I took it down and put it on. It was far too big so I wound my plaits around my head then fitted it on top. Something moved near the window and I saw the melon vine, or whatever it was, had grown over the panes like a curtain, and the shine-moth was fluttering against the glass. I opened the window and pulled the vine aside and the moth flew straight up into the air until it was a speck high above Spit Farm.

Pop was in the ground by the time I returned to the clearing and each person was putting a shovelful of dirt on top of him. The goat bells had been set to one side.

I took off my grandfather's hat and held it in front of

me. Some of the cousins were kneeling and there were sighs of regret. I wondered why they sighed like that when they hardly knew Pop.

It was turning dark by the time the hole was filled. Oma patted the earth down on top, then she stood up and addressed the crowd.

'There was no better man this side of the Palisades,' she said. 'He sang a good song and his heart was big as the mountain.' Her voice wobbled a bit and Vern took her arm.

'Goodbye, Ort,' she said.

After that we went back home, and Oma lit the bonfire.

'Was that button-box always under the bed?' I asked her. 'How come Pop never played it before?'

Oma looked very tired. She put her hands on my shoulders.

'Ellie, it's gone now. I don't want to speak of it and you mustn't either.'

'But—'

'No buts. The subject is closed. Go and help Lil bring out the food.'

'Did you know about the button-box, Auntie Lil?' I asked when I reached the shack. 'Did Pop always have it?'

'I don't know. It was in the family. Like lots of things.'

She handed me a stack of hoe cakes on a tin plate.

'Where did it come from?' I asked.

'It's not our business, Ellie.'

'Did you know what it could do?'

My auntie shrugged. 'Leave it,' she said. 'Go and enjoy the party.'

The music was soft at first but it grew boisterous as the evening went on. I didn't like to think of Pop lying alone up there in the clearing. When the dancing started I decided to go to him.

I headed up the path. The night was cold and my breath made little white clouds in front of me. The sound of the wake faded and soon all I could hear was my footfalls as I walked through the pine needles.

When I saw the lawyer in the clearing I stopped dead. His head was down and he held his cap in his hands but he didn't look sad. He was smiling to himself and mumbling.

'Be doing everyone a favour...' he said.

He looked up and addressed the tree he'd been leaning on. 'Your honour, it's a criminal waste to bury an instrument like that. It has power, the power to melt a mountain – I witnessed it myself!' He swayed slightly then he cleared his throat and drew himself up to his full height.

'The client's express wishes were that it be buried with him but the will was never signed.' He burst out laughing and this made him stagger. He dropped his satchel on the ground then he reached for the shovel near his feet and started digging.

I stepped behind a tree and held my breath, horrified. He was so drunk he could barely stand but he managed to heap aside the dirt. When he'd uncovered the burial box he threw away the shovel and leaned into the hole. The lid came off easily. He put it aside, then reached down and took the instrument from Pop's hands. They must have been stiff because he had to struggle to get it free.

'It's mine!' he cried as he pulled the button-box towards him.

I was frozen to the spot. I knew he shouldn't be doing that. How dare he! I thought of running back to get Oma or Uncle Vern and I was about to leave when the lawyer stood up. He put the strap of the button-box over his shoulder then he picked up his satchel and lurched towards his horse. It took him several tries to get mounted because his foot kept slipping from the stirrup and once he was in the saddle he leaned danger-ously to one side. The button-box swung forward and frightened the horse, which took off at full gallop. It swept past me, heading towards Jutt Rock, and when it was almost there it disappeared down the mountain-side. The country was steep and dangerous. Below Jutt Rock were scree slopes and a boulder field that ended in a sheer drop.

'No!' I yelled. 'Stop!'

I don't think the lawyer heard me and even if he did, he couldn't control the horse. I ran after them.

When I reached Jutt Rock I paused to catch my breath and looked down. The moon was up and the rocky hillside shone in its light. There was no sign of the lawyer.

I was sure the horse had gone over the edge. Then

I heard a sound, the faint echo of hoofbeats clattering on stone. Something moved between the boulders far below, then the hoofbeats grew louder and the horse appeared, riderless and following a narrow path that wound back up the slope towards me.

It was panting hard and lathered in sweat. I tried to catch hold of the reins as it passed but it shied away and disappeared into the forest. I stood for a few moments, my chest heaving in shock.

Then I remembered Pop, lying with the lid off his burial box.

I returned to the clearing and put it back in place. After that, I filled the hole and knelt down, patting the earth smooth, the way Oma had. My heart was still beating fast, but there was heaviness there, too. When I'd finished I sat by the side of Pop's grave and hugged my knees. It was hard to believe he was gone. I'd never sit by his bed again. I'd never tell him stories that would make him laugh. Tears rolled down my cheeks and dripped off my chin.

'Goodbye, Pop,' I whispered.

4

The Button-box

'THERE WAS ONCE a herd of fabulous goats. They were tall and strong and they lived in the Gleam country west of the Palisades. Their fleece was softer than clouds and so fine even the slightest garment made from it would keep you warm all winter. What a land they lived in! It was a place of sweet grass and endless streams and the people there were wise and kind and they would never disturb a grave.'

I pressed my face into Nanny Gitto's flank as I milked her. I hadn't told Oma what had happened after the funeral. She'd have been so upset. And I knew if I told my brother he'd tell Oma. So I didn't tell anyone except Nanny Gitto.

'The girl who looked after the herd was called Gola. She was sure-footed as a mountain goat and her hair hung down her back in two pale tresses. Her best friend's name was Gabe. He was a goatherd too and everyone knew that when Gola reached her promise age he was the one she would choose. They had played together when they were little and they were still playing, laughing and joking, and the mountains rang with the sound of their voices. Do you like the story, Nanny?'

Nanny lifted her head from the feed trough and stared at me. Usually when I told her stories she kept eating. She gave me a piercing look and there was something accusing in her gaze.

'Nanny, what is it?'

Nanny didn't reply. I didn't expect her to. I used to imagine that creatures spoke to me when I was little, until Oma told me to stop being silly.

Nanny kept staring.

I thought of the lawyer's horse. It was probably halfway to Fel's Hollow by now. I hoped its reins hadn't got tangled in anything. Then I pictured the lawyer. It seemed obvious what had happened: the horse had stopped in time but the lawyer had gone over the edge. Suddenly I had a shocking thought – what if the man hadn't died?

I stopped milking and gulped. It was as if Nanny had put that idea in my mind by looking at me so sharply.

What if Strand was lying somewhere among the boulders? What if he'd been there, badly injured, all night?

Nanny stared at me with her golden eyes, then abruptly put her head back in the feed trough and kept eating. I began milking again and tried to put the lawyer out of my mind. There was no way he could have survived that fall. I continued with the story.

'And when the promise day came the wedding was held in the cave where Gola kept her goats. Everyone came and they danced for days, which would have been months or even years in our world.'

I squeezed the last of the milk out of Nanny's teat and began on the other.

'After the wedding, Gola and Gabe went and lived on top of Shine Mountain. They had three beautiful babies and they were happy forever.'

I was trying to think of the names of the babies when Tod opened the barn door.

'The last lot is leaving,' he said. 'Going before the weather turns. If it turns. It's like spring out here, warmer outside than in. Do you want to say goodbye to Wade?'

I finished milking and went out. Most of the relatives had left before dawn. Wade was one of the last to go.

'Look after yourself, Ellie West,' he said. 'If you're ever down my way, call in and see me.' He shook my hand as if I was the sort of person who might head off to the plains at the drop of a hat. As far as I knew Pop was the only person in our family who'd been there.

I watched him walk up Bald Hill towards the pass then I got the dogs and took the goats out, telling Oma I'd be gone all day. I hurried towards Jutt Rock.

It was a clear morning and the snow on the high slopes had melted. When I reached Jutt the goats fanned out and began browsing. I stood on the rock, looking down. I could see the curvy silver line of Spit River far below. Closer to home was the scree slope.

I decided the goats would be all right left alone and headed downhill, looking for the track. The dogs came with me. Their names were Mooti and Gus and they were from Elsie's litter. Elsie was our best follow-dog. She'd stay on your heels all day, but she could also work alone, and more than once she'd protected our goats from marauding scavenger-hounds. She'd even attacked a range-cat once when it tried to take a kid. The cat was three times her size but Elsie had driven it off.

I was glad I had the dogs. I didn't want to find Alexis Strand by myself.

I hadn't gone far when I saw papers laying on the ground: Pop's will – I recognised the lawyer's spidery writing. Further on I found the satchel. I guess he dropped it. He would have needed to hang on with both hands.

I found a track and almost immediately saw something on the path ahead: a leather strap. One end was attached by a stud to a piece of splintered wood. There was a burn mark on one side and I could see a leaf pattern and a row of holes. It was part of the button-box. Nearby was a tiny white rod. It fitted exactly in one of the holes, so I knew it was a button. When I picked it up, Mooti growled.

There were more bits scattered about – flat pieces of brass, little metal levers and a carved piece of wood that had radiating spokes like a sun.

I looked downhill. I could see something a long way off, a bit of black cloth caught on a pole.

'Come on, Mooti,' I said.

She fixed me with a blank stare and wouldn't budge. Gus was the same. He sat down and looked the other way.

There's a stubbornness to Spit Farm animals, and to the people as well, which could be due to breeding or the weather or the hard country. Even Pop, who was a gentle-natured man, had a flinty streak in him when he got a set on something.

'Come on!' I yelled.

Mooti and Gus stayed where they were. I left the path and made my way over the rocks. In some places I had to clamber over boulders, my hook foot catching with each step. The way grew steep and somehow I lost my balance. I heard Mooti howl as I tumbled down the slope and it was pure luck when my toe snagged on the pole, pulling me up short with a jolt. It was an old ironwood pole that might have been used as a trail marker when the snow was deep. My bad foot snagged, and that's what saved me – if it had been the other one, my ankle would have flexed and I would have gone over the edge, because that's what gaped before me, not three paces from the pole. The bit of cloth was part of the lawyer's oilskin jacket. I could have crawled forward and looked over, but I didn't dare.

I picked myself up and scrambled back to the dogs, my heart hammering in my chest. Once I was on the path I put all the bits of the button-box into the lawyer's satchel and hurried to the goats. When I reached the top of the slope I hid the satchel in a hollow log. Nanny was curious and came to look. She sniffed the log and gave a startled cry. Then she backed away.

Nanny Gitto was a calm and sensible goat. It was unusual for her to behave that way. Suddenly she turned and fled towards home, bleating wildly, and the herd followed.

'What on earth's going on?' Oma asked when I arrived back.

'Nothing. Nanny got a fright, that's all.'

The goats nosed around the shack and Nanny scratched her head on the verandah post as if nothing had happened.

I told Oma I'd take the goats back but I didn't take them all the way. Instead I let them graze in the open country north of the yards and went on by myself to Pop's grave. There were sunflowers growing on it. They'd sprung up overnight.

I wished I'd asked Pop things when he was alive. There was no point in asking him now, but I did anyway.

'Did you always have that button-box under the bed, Pop? Where did it come from?'

There was no answer except for the wind in the trees.

5

The Lost Kid

IT FELT LIKE SPRING. It *was* spring. Pop was three days dead and the fruit trees were suddenly in bud, the snow had gone and the vine over the window had flowers on it that looked like trumpets. Uncle Vern decided to take advantage of the strange weather and put in a new garden bed. He diverted a silted-up stream down by the wash. The earth was good but no use down there where the sun never shone. It had to be brought up near the shack, and as the slope was too steep for the ponies the only way to transport it was on our backs.

Auntie Shirl told me to get a basket from the barn and I followed her down the wash-path. Oma was already there, digging out soil for the next load.

We were almost at the wash when a calf bawled somewhere from the direction of the pass. It wasn't one of ours. My aunt paused and looked up.

'Herders!' She spat out the word. 'You'd think they

owned the world. I'll set the dogs on them if they bring their stock anywhere near the top pastures. We've got little enough feed as it is.'

That wasn't true. With the snow melted, a green pick covered the hills. Besides, the slopes where we grazed the goats weren't part of Spit Farm so the herders had just as much right to them as we did.

'If any of them come sniffing around, send them away. They'll take anything that's not nailed down.'

Shirl scowled in the direction of the pass then kept trudging down the hill.

'Hurry up, Ellie. We haven't got all day.'

I decided to ask my aunt about the button-box, though I knew that was a foolish thing to do. Shirley Serpentine had never liked me, and now that Pop was gone she didn't try to hide it.

'Did you ever see it before?'

'Never clamped eyes on it. But I heard of it.'

'What did you hear?'

'Nothing for your ears.'

When we reached the stream she took the shovel from Oma's hands.

'Turn about,' she told me. She began filling my basket, giving a satisfied grunt as each shovel load landed with a thud.

'You're going to have trouble with her, Flo,' she said. 'She's nosey as a rat in a feedbin.'

Shirl spoke as if I wasn't there. Oma bit her lip. I could tell she was making an effort not to argue in front of me.

Oma and Shirl had never got on. They used to snap at each other but now they were arguing every day. It was never about anything important: whether to plant beans or cabbage, whether to put in the corn now or wait until later in the season. My presence seemed to make it worse.

'Half is enough, Shirl,' my grandmother said. 'She's not full grown.'

Oma had told me that my aunt couldn't help being the way she was. She'd swallowed something bitter in her youth and never got it out of her system. I couldn't imagine Shirley Serpentine ever being young. She had a face that could dry up a well with a single glance and that's why Oma kept her away from the goats – she didn't want them losing their milk. Shirl and Uncle Vern mostly ate their meals separately, which Pop always said was a waste because it meant two lots of fuel and two lots of cooking.

Oma's mouth was set in a hard line. 'Ellie, when you get this load to the top, go and get your brother. He's out Jutt way.'

I grabbed a stick and headed off, my legs trembling as I scrambled up the steep slope. Once I'd made it to the top I tipped my dirt on the heap and kept going towards Jutt Rock. The dogs barked and came to greet me.

'Shirl again?' my brother asked.

I nodded. 'They're carting dirt. The basket's on the heap.'

Tod was happy to go; he'd rather carry dirt than

mind the goats. Once he left I went to the log and took out the lawyer's satchel.

'Come Mooti. Come Gus.'

The dogs followed me down the track between the boulders but when I reached the place where I'd found the pieces of the button-box they lay down and whined, refusing to go any further.

'Cuss hounds! Your ma would be ashamed of you!' I didn't normally curse the dogs but they annoyed me that day.

I continued on alone and spent all afternoon looking on the track. I found valves and springs and more buttons, and then I came across a piece of wood with leaf-shapes cut from it. It was the other end of the instrument. The bellows were attached – half a dozen folds, which ended in a ragged tear.

I laid everything out on a flat rock, wondering how it might fit together. The buttons filled the holes and the piece of wood with the spokes fitted exactly at the open end of the bellows, but I had no idea where to put the other bits.

When I looked up I was surprised to see the sun disappearing behind Bald Hill. I quickly put everything in the satchel and hurried back to the goats. But when I reached the spot where I'd left them, they were nowhere to be seen. Tod was sitting on my log with his back to me. I quickly hid the satchel behind a rock.

'You're in big trouble, Sis.' He pointed to the ground in front of him. 'Just look at that!'

It was a kid, or the remains of one. There wasn't much left, just the head and a bit of skin.

'Scavenger-hound?' I whispered.

'Uncle Vern found the rest of the herd in Fel's Hollow. He's taken them home. Where have you been?'

'I was picking wilderberries.' It was the first thing I could think of.

Tod knew as well as I did that wilderberries didn't grow out this way.

'Why are you fibbing?' he said.

My face felt hot and I couldn't meet his eyes. We walked home in silence.

Our herd wasn't so big that we could afford to lose an animal. Every goat was precious. Perhaps I should have taken the loss of the kid as a sign and left the button-box alone. I could have put the parts back where I found them and forgotten all about it, but I didn't.

6

The Tinker

WHEN WE GOT BACK there was a handcart standing outside Vern and Shirl's shed. It was loaded with saucepans and skillets. A cow with bony hips and corrugated sides was tied to the back of it and a calf was nosing about near the barn. A dusty-looking man leaned on the cart with his arms folded while his wife argued with Shirl, who stood in the doorway, one hand on her hip and the other on her shotgun.

'Get on your way. We've got nothing for you.'

'He's not asking for much. Just a pot to mend.'

Oma sat on the verandah with her legs stretched out in front of her, a skein of wool around her feet. She was pulling the wool off and winding it into a ball. I went and sat next to her.

'Never leave the goats, Ellie.'

'I'm sorry, Oma.'

'Where was Mooti?'

'She was with me.'

'Keep your livestock away!' Shirl yelled to the tinker, noticing the calf.

The man picked up the shafts of his cart. 'Come on, Maude,' he said. 'Leave it.'

I took the wool and looped it over my hands, keeping them apart to hold the tension. Oma wound faster. She watched the couple trudge away, the little calf trotting behind.

Shirl spat and went into her shed, slamming the door behind her.

I could hear the clinking of the tinker's pots and wondered where they would spend the night.

Oma finished winding up the wool. 'Wait here,' she said.

She went inside, returning with a frypan with a broken handle and a rusty bucket that we used to keep down at the wash before it started leaking. She'd put a flour bag half full of grain in it.

'Go after them and give them these. Tell them you'll come back tomorrow to collect them. Take the back way so Shirl doesn't see you.'

I followed the sound of the handcart and caught up with the couple in the scrub behind the yards. A wagon was parked there. It had wooden sides and a tarp over the top. A mule was tethered to a tree nearby. It was bony like the cow.

'There's grass further on,' I told them, as I handed over the things that needed mending. 'Keep going till you find the track that leads to the slopes. You could tether your mule there.'

The man glanced at my foot and nodded his thanks. The woman said nothing. She had a weather-beaten face and her dress was faded to no colour. She looked worn out. She untied the mule and led him away.

The man opened a box in his handcart and took out tin snips and pliers.

'That's a big hat for a small girl,' he said. 'What do they call you?'

'Ellie.'

He took out a piece of bent tin and beat it flat.

'I'll have to fashion a new handle for the pan.'

He opened the back of the wagon and brought out a straw broom, then he cut a hand's length off the end of the broomstick and drilled a hole in it. As he rummaged in the box in his handcart looking for a bolt the right size, I peered inside the wagon. There was a narrow bed, a work bench and a wall full of delicate tools: tongs, punches, a tiny hammer and a pair of little tweezers.

'Are they for the pot work?' I asked.

'Jewellery,' he said. 'There's not much call for it up this way but we do good trade in the lowland towns.' He reached into the wagon and brought out a box of coloured stones.

'Not valuable,' he said, 'but they look pretty.'

There was a brooch in among them, a flower fashioned in tin with a blue stone in its centre.

'Do you have any good rocks around here?'

I shook my head. The only nice stones I'd ever seen were in the necklace that had been left to Lil in Pop's will. Pop once said the stones were meant to be lucky.

I watched the man use his snips to cut a circle of tin. He fitted it inside the bottom of the bucket then he put in rivets and soldered the edge to make a neat join.

'Can you fix other things?' I asked. 'I have something else. I'll bring it tomorrow. I'll bring more food as well.'

The next morning I got up early and collected the satchel. As soon as I'd finished my chores I hurried to the tinker's camp. The woman was cooking over a fire. She stood up and took the oatbread and eggs that I'd brought.

'Precious, is it?' she asked, noticing how I clutched the bag to my chest. 'He's inside.'

She followed me into the wagon and watched as I put the pieces on the table.

'It's only a busted button-box.' She shook her head and went back to the fire.

Her husband was more interested.

'It's cunningly crafted,' he said. 'The buttons are carved from bone.'

He examined the bellows, then picked up a lever and studied it. 'I'm not sure I can mend this. I wouldn't know where to start.'

'Please,' I begged. 'Just see if you can put it back together.'

He picked up the bit of wood with the hand strap attached. 'There's borers in the fretwork. I could try and make a new grille for the front of it but I'd have to make it out of tin. It might rattle a bit.'

The man pulled up a stool. 'It could take me a week,' he muttered. 'And it would probably sound worse than a braying donkey.'

I offered to take their mule out to graze. That would be some payment. Already I was thinking how much food I could take from the holdfast without anyone noticing. I led the mule up to the grassy slopes, staying out of sight of the shack and hoping I wouldn't be missed. After an hour or two I returned to find the tinker still sitting at his table. He had straightened the bent levers, patched and oiled the bellows and fitted the back plate on.

'I can't figure how the stoppers fit,' he said. 'You'll have to leave this instrument with me.'

'I can't leave it.'

He looked at the bits and pieces on his table and then looked at me.

'Tell you what, I'll take it off your hands. I'll buy it.'

'What? That piece of junk?' His wife leaned in the door of the wagon. 'Don't be ridiculous.'

'I can't sell it,' I cried. 'It used to belong to my pop.'

'Well, how about you bring us some more things from your house and he'll see what he can do?' The woman stood with her arms crossed, waiting for me to go.

I didn't like leaving the button-box but there wasn't much choice. As I walked away I heard the tinker's wife tell him he was wasting his time.

'You'll get nothing out of this job. I say we leave tomorrow.'

'You shouldn't be asking the girl to rob her own family,' he countered.

I didn't think taking food to pay the tinker was robbing, but I suppose it was, and by the time I reached the shack I'd come up with a better idea. I desperately wanted that button-box fixed. I wanted to play it like Pop had. It occurred to me that my Auntie Lil wouldn't miss that white necklace. Nobody would even notice it was gone.

I returned the next day with it in my pocket.

'It's moonstone.' I said. 'It's very old and very valuable.'

I really had no idea if it was valuable or not, but from the way the lady stared at the stones I thought it might be.

'You could make each rock into a ring,' I suggested. 'There's twenty-four of them.'

It took the tinker three days to fix the instrument. He'd put everything back inside it and he'd fashioned a new hook for the front so it could close up tight. The only sound it made was a wheezing intake of air and the clacking of the spring-loaded buttons as they went up and down. The bellows creaked slightly and the tin plate on the front rattled.

'The reeds are missing,' he explained. 'The wind's going in but there's nothing to vibrate. That's as much as I can do.'

I gave him the necklace and put the button-box in

the satchel. I wasn't bothered by the fact that it wouldn't play; to have it put together was enough. Maybe one day I'd get it fixed properly.

I thanked the man and headed off.

꩜

I NEEDED A good safe place to store my treasure.

There was a cave below the wash that had once been used to store potatoes. Tod and I played there when we were small. We called it the shade-cave and we went there to make secret wishes.

'At the back?' I asked.

I never got answers to my questions, not the sort that you could hear, but sometimes I got pictures and as I leaned against the railing with the button-box on my lap I saw a passage at the back of the cave. It must have always been there but I'd never seen it.

'Perfect!' I said, and hurried on.

One of the chooks followed me when I passed the hen house – a pet I called Fat Hattie because of her size and the tuft of dark feathers sprouting from the back of her head. She had stopped laying a long time ago but Oma let me keep her. I picked her up and carried her, taking a handful of oats from the feed shed as I passed to keep her happy.

'No one will miss the necklace,' I told her. 'Certainly not Auntie Lil.'

The hen looked at me with her beady eye and blinked, taking it in. It was good to have someone to tell.

'There's no reason to feel guilty, Hat.'

She made a little crooning noise as if she agreed.

The opening to the cave was overgrown. Nobody went there anymore. It was as good a place as any to store my treasure and it wasn't far from home. I set Hattie down and she watched me take out the button-box. A shaft of late afternoon sunlight fell through the entrance and made the tin grille gleam. The instrument was a thing of beauty and promise. I was proud to have saved it. If it had been left on the scree slope it would have been lost for good.

I scattered the oats for my hen and she scratched around and pecked as I undid the hook and slipped my hands under the straps. When I extended the bellows, Hattie looked up. The button-box gave a gasp as if it was struggling for breath. Then it took off! That's the only way I can describe it. The buttons moved up and down, taking my fingers with them, and I found my arms pumping hard. I heard nothing except the clacking noise of the springs and a rhythmic wheeze that sounded like panting. And then I had a strange sensation: I felt someone was moving towards me, rushing through the dark reaches of the cave. I looked over my shoulder but nobody was there.

I quickly squeezed the bellows shut and put the hook back in place. My heart was thudding in my ears and my fingers tingled.

'Who's there?' I cried.

There was movement outside and a shadow fell across the entrance.

I held my breath and kept perfectly still. Hattie began scratching and scuffling. She kicked some oats outside and clucked quietly to herself as she followed them.

'What's *she* doing here!' Tod stuck his head into the cave. 'Caught you,' he crowed. 'I thought you were too big for wishes!' Then his eyes fell on the button-box and a look of bewilderment filled his face.

'That's Pop's. You shouldn't... I'm telling—'

He turned and ran, crashing through the ferns.

'No, Tod, wait! Come back.'

He was halfway to the wash before I caught up with him.

'I found it, Tod. I found all the bits and the tinker man fixed it.'

'Found it where? It was in the box with Pop.'

'That fellow – the lawyer – he took it out again.'

'What are you talking about?'

'It's magic, Tod. Let me show you.'

'I know that,' he said. 'We saw what it could do.'

I led him back to the shade-cave and it was almost dark when we went inside. Fat Hattie was still scratching by the entrance.

I told my brother everything and he listened in silence. When I'd finished he reached for the instrument.

'Do you think it still works?' he asked.

'I don't know. It gave me a funny feeling.'

'We need to know the song,' he said.

'What song?'

'Pop's song. It won't work without the song.' He

thought for a moment. 'Something…something… *mountain girl when spring is in the air…*' He sang the words then paused. 'You play and I'll sing.'

I cautiously picked up the instrument. Fat Hattie came and sat in front of me. She cocked her head and watched as I opened the bellows.

'What comes next…? *Her skin glows soft as blossom and flowers bloom in her hair.*'

Tod had a better memory than me. He hummed the bits he didn't know and I played the instrument, or perhaps I should say the instrument played me, because I didn't feel I was in charge. My fingers buzzed and I had a rushing sensation.

Fat Hattie closed her eyes as if she was listening to every note, and when the song ended her comb was red and standing up. The combs of chickens look like that when they're young and laying. Fat Hattie's had been pale and wilted for more than a year. Suddenly she cackled loudly. I thought that might be her way of applauding, but when she stood up I saw she'd laid an egg. She preened her breast feathers and walked away. I dropped the button-box in surprise. It landed on my lap and the bellows stretched open, making a groaning sound that ended in a sigh.

I stared at the egg. Tod's mouth fell open and then a smile spread across his face.

'It works!' he cried. But he looked doubtful.

He picked up the egg and examined it. 'I don't know, Sis. I don't think it's right. I think the button-box should go back to where it's meant to be. Let's go and see Oma.'

'What? It can't go back in with Pop! Please, Tod. Don't tell.'

I squeezed the button-box shut and put it back in the satchel. Then I tucked Fat Hattie under my arm and we headed home.

7

Heat Wave

THERE WAS NO light on in the shack when we got back. Normally Oma would be inside cooking.

'She's poorly,' Shirley Serpentine yelled across the yard. 'You're to eat with us tonight.'

Auntie Lil was sitting outside Shirl's shed, knitting.

'What's wrong?' I asked. Oma had never been sick before.

Auntie Lil didn't answer. She went into the shed, returning with two bowls of soup, which she handed to me.

'Go and see her, Ellie.'

I hurried over to the porch.

'Oma, are you all right?' I called.

'Just fine.' She spoke from the back room.

'Why are you in the dark? Are you in bed?'

I put the bowls down on the bench and lit a lamp.

'Just bring the food in and leave the light outside.'

She spoke softly and there was something strange about her voice. She didn't sound ill or weak. I took the soup into the back room. She was sitting on our palliasse with a shawl over her head. 'Oma, are you cold? What's wrong?'

'Shut the door.'

I did as she asked and then I couldn't see her at all. I held out the bowl and she took it then I sat beside her and we both ate. When she'd finished she put the bowl aside.

'I don't feel myself, El.'

'You're sick?'

'Not at all.' She reached out and patted my knee, then she put her arm around me and she felt different somehow, not as soft as she usually was. She smelt of orange blossom and sweet plums.

'Feel this.'

She pulled off the shawl and took my hand and placed it on her head. Her hair felt strange. It was soft and springy. I caught my breath.

'Oma, you know how I lost the kid?' My voice wavered. She squeezed me tight and again I felt how different she was; there was less of her but she was stronger.

'It's been on your mind. That's why you've been acting strangely. Let me tell you, girl, it's not the first time a goat's been lost and it won't be the last.'

'It's not that...'

I suddenly wanted to tell Oma what I'd done – how I'd left the goats and gone looking for the lawyer, and how I'd found the button-box instead. I was about to speak when Auntie Lil arrived.

'How are you feeling, Flo?' She opened the door and as Oma threw the shawl back over her head I caught a glimpse of a woman I barely recognised, a young woman.

'Quite all right. It's probably a passing thing. We'll talk about it in the morning.'

⁂

I HARDLY SLEPT that night and I was up before dawn. Auntie Lil was still asleep and I think Oma was too. She was facing the wall and her shawl was still over her head. I wanted to get to the cave as soon as I could. Don't ask me why – I just wanted to see the button-box. Fat Hattie was sitting on the doorstep of the porch as if she was waiting for me. And Tod was too. He was leading Sol.

'Look!' he whispered, pointing to the garden. The beans that Auntie Shirl had planted in the new bed were as high as my knee. They hadn't been up the day before. I stared in surprise and, scooping Hattie under my arm, headed off with Tod on my heels.

'Is Oma all right?' he asked.

'She's got younger,' I said, when we were away from the shack.

'What?' He grabbed my arm.

'There's no harm in it, Tod. She looks a bit different, that's all.'

My brother climbed on Sol and pulled me up after him.

The sun had risen by the time we reached the wash. When I looked down the slope towards the cave I couldn't believe my eyes. Long green grass grew up through the ferns in front of the entrance. It hadn't been there yesterday. Sol broke into a trot and as we came closer I saw it was oats. They grew tall and thick and each stem was bowed with the weight of the grain. I bit into one and tasted the milky sweetness. Sol began eating. Tod slid down his neck and landed among them.

'We've never had a crop like this before!' he cried, his arms outstretched.

I couldn't help laughing and Tod laughed too, although he looked a bit worried.

The oats made a green curtain in front of the cave. It occurred to me that if anyone looked down from the wash they would notice the entrance, so I jumped off and started pulling them out, grabbing handfuls of stalks and uprooting them.

'Don't, El!' Tod jumped on my back and clung there, laughing. I tried to tip him off and we started wrestling. It was half play and half serious, and in the end we fell on our backs, panting and looking up through the oats in silence. The only sound was Sol munching. Then I heard rustling. Fat Hattie was pushing her way into the cave.

'Come on,' I cried. 'Let's do it again!'

The oats were thicker inside the entrance than out and we had to search to find the satchel, trampling an area flat in the process. I sat down and took out the button-box. Tod remained standing.

'Do you think we should?' he asked.

'What are you scared of?'

'Nothing.'

When I slipped my hands under the straps the button-box felt familiar. The bellows opened automatically; in and out they went, and the buttons clacked up and down, moving my fingers.

'Sing, Tod!' I yelled.

My brother kept silent so I closed my eyes and tried to remember the words, but I couldn't think because of the rushing in my mind. Again I felt somebody moving towards me. The panting of the bellows was like a person breathing, and I have to admit it frightened me. Outside, I heard Sol neigh. I looked down at my hands. They might have belonged to someone else. My fingers were moving so fast I could barely see them.

'Stop!' Tod yelled. He put his hands over mine and together we forced the button-box closed. I held it shut while he slipped the catch.

There was no applause this time, no cackling from my hen. She gave a little croak and lowered her beak.

Tod let go of me and swept his hands through the oats around him as if he was trying to wipe something off them. The stalks were dry and the oats rattled. Some fell on the ground in front of Hattie but she didn't pick them up. Her feathers looked tatty and her comb was grey and wrinkled.

I put my head close to hers. 'What is it, Hattie?

What's wrong?' That strange dry eyelid that fowls have closed like a window and Hattie dropped her head. For a moment I thought she was dead. Then she stood up and began pecking the oats as if nothing had happened.

'Let's go.' I suddenly wanted to get away. The sun was well and truly up and I realised I'd lost track of time; Oma would be waiting for me to help with the milking. It was Tod's turn to take the goats out when we finished.

'We won't speak of this,' I said. 'Spit on your hand and swear?'

We both spat and shook hands and then I picked Hattie up and we climbed onto Sol. I didn't bother putting the button-box back in the satchel. As we headed up the hill, I was glad to leave it behind.

When we got back, Auntie Lil and Shirl Serpentine were watering the garden, filling buckets from the trough by the back door. They didn't comment on us being late.

'I can't understand it. The beans grew up overnight and now they're wilting.' Shirl looked at us. 'Don't just stand there. Grab a bucket.'

'The squash are drying up as well,' said Auntie Lil. 'And the potatoes and corn need watering.'

Oma was coming back from the barn, having finished the milking. She had a bucket in each hand and was walking slowly. I ran to her and took the milk. She looked a little tired but apart from that she seemed her usual self. She wasn't wearing the shawl.

'A sudden heat wave, Ellie,' she said. 'I don't know where it's come from.'

Tod went off with the goats and I took the milk inside. Then I helped Oma strap the waterbags on the ponies. We went down to the spring and refilled the trough outside the shack. We were on our second trip when Shirl joined us.

'It's like the middle of summer.' Sweat poured down her face and she wiped her brow and looked about as if she was searching for someone to blame. Her gaze rested on me.

'I wouldn't be surprised if this is her doing.'

'Oh, Shirl,' Oma sighed. 'Don't start that again.'

Shirley Serpentine stared at my boot. She always believed my foot was bad luck and whenever things weren't going right she'd say, 'It's that foot that's caused this.'

Oma didn't reply. She filled her bucket and handed it to me and I emptied it into the waterbag.

'That will about do me for the day,' my grandmother sighed, grabbing a handful of the pony's mane. She clicked her tongue and let the pony drag her up the bank. I followed along behind.

'Are you all right, Oma?'

'Just a little weary.'

When we had emptied the bags she sat on the edge of the trough and caught her breath.

'We're probably wasting our energy,' she said. 'It could rain in the next couple of days.'

IT DIDN'T RAIN, not in the next couple of days or the next week or the week after that. Tod and I spent our time carting water. It was so hot that we sheared the goats because the weather was distressing them. Oma said she didn't feel up to making the journey to the Trading Post to sell the wool, so Auntie Shirl went. Oma had begun to look her age, whatever that was.

I had never thought of Oma being old but now I had to believe it. Her skin was dry and papery and her hair grew wispy.

Despite our careful watering, the beans died straight after they flowered, and when the tops of the potatoes withered Auntie Lil dug under them and found nothing there. I wished I'd harvested those oats before I pulled them out.

Oma tried not to look worried. 'Once the rain comes we'll replant the garden,' she said.

Auntie Shirl came back from the Trading Post with a bag of grain.

'We'll have to make this last,' she said. 'No double dipping. And Ellie, you're not to waste it on the hens.'

The warm weather continued. It was supposed to be winter but it grew hotter every day. There was no rain and the grass on the slopes behind the shack dried off. We had to take the goats further to graze. This wore on them and they gave less milk and got a ragged look.

Even Nanny Gitto grew scraggy. She normally gave a full pail of milk each day but now she was down to half.

'It's a bad season,' Uncle Vern said. 'But there's been droughts before.' He kept his eye on the sky, looking for clouds.

'If this keeps up we'll be eating pea straw from the palliasse,' Auntie Shirl remarked. 'It hasn't been this bad since the year Ellie was born.'

They'd been short of food that year and Shirl had gone away to work because the farm couldn't support everyone. She'd spoken of it often, always with an accusing glance in my direction. She'd got a job in Scarp, on the Sidling Road.

Soon there was nothing left in the garden and the water that normally bubbled up quickly at the spring had slowed, so we had to wait while the scoop-pool refilled before bucketing into the waterbags. Oma didn't come to help anymore. The work was too heavy for her.

A month passed and there was still no sign of rain. By then we'd used up most of the grain.

'We still have meat and eggs and milk,' Oma said.

Auntie Lil was worried. She decided she would sell her necklace and use the money to buy food.

'We won't get its full value from the Trading Post,' she said. 'But what else can we do?'

She was surprised to find that the necklace wasn't in its usual place on the mantelpiece.

'Perhaps I put it away somewhere,' Oma said. 'I'm getting absent-minded.'

She searched in the kitchen drawer and I pretended to help while Shirley stood in the doorway, watching with her arms folded.

'I bet those tinkers took it,' she said. 'Ellie shouldn't have encouraged them, going up to their camp like that. I expect that woman came back and pinched it when nobody was about.'

'It's my fault,' Oma sighed. 'I shouldn't have given them work.'

My face went red and I looked away.

8

Alma West

'YOU'RE NOT KIN,' Shirl said one day when we were in the holdfast taking down the last of our salt pork. 'I've always suspected it and now I'm sure. Not with that foot and your strange ways. You don't belong here.'

I tried not to take any notice of her, but it upset me. That night when we were in bed I told Oma.

'She's full of wild imaginings,' my grandmother said. 'She makes up stories and then she believes they're true.'

The moon shone through the window onto Oma's face and I touched her forehead, smoothing out the wrinkles.

'Laughter lines,' she said, and that made my throat tight because I realised Oma hadn't laughed since Pop died. 'While I think of it, you might put your hen somewhere safe. Now that the meat's run out Shirl wants to start killing the fowls.'

'Fat Hattie died.'

Oma sat up. 'When?'

'A week ago.'

'Why didn't you tell me?'

When I didn't answer, Oma took my hand. 'Your hen was old, Ellie. I'm surprised she lived as long as she did.'

'It was my fault.' Suddenly I couldn't bear it any longer. 'It's all my fault, Oma – Fat Hattie, this dry weather, and whatever's happening to you.'

'Hush, child, that's Shirley Serpentine talking.' Oma squeezed my hand. 'I'm going to have a word with that woman. I'm going to put an end to this nonsense about your foot.'

At dinner the next evening, Auntie Shirl gave her the perfect opportunity. Uncle Vern was talking about the fowls.

'We should keep them,' he said. 'They'll start laying again as soon as the rains come.'

'We shouldn't be in this situation.' Shirl looked at me. 'Didn't I always say it would go this way?'

Oma told Tod and me to take our meals outside. The goats were hanging around in front of the shack hoping to be fed and when we sat down on the verandah with our backs against the wall, Nanny Gitto came and nibbled at our boots. I stroked her ears, straining to hear the argument inside.

'It's the fault of the girl,' Shirley said.

We couldn't hear Oma's reply.

'That's not true,' Tod whispered. 'It's my fault as much as yours.'

'I'm the one who started it. If Oma dies like Hattie it'll be my fault.'

He turned to me, wide-eyed. 'Why would Oma die?'

I stopped stroking Nanny.

'Oh Tod, can't you see what's happening to her?'

We couldn't hear what the adults were saying so we crept around the side of the shack and sat below the kitchen window, wedging ourselves between the water trough and the wall where we couldn't be seen if anyone looked out. Nanny followed.

'Claptrap!' Oma yelled. 'You're a fool to believe such rubbish!'

'Fool or no fool, I bet if she leaves, things will improve.'

'Remember the kid we had with the turned hoof?' Uncle Vern's voice was steady. 'She grew up and had five kids herself. There's no bad luck in that. All this will blow over like the weather.'

'I'm not sending her away, Shirl. How dare you suggest it,' Oma cried.

'We haven't enough food to see us through, not all of us. If Ellie goes she'll take the problems with her. We've relatives in Scarp. She could stay with them.'

Something crashed onto the kitchen floor and then the back door swung open. Nanny skittered away in fright and then she watched Oma stumble outside. My grandmother felt around for the stick she'd taken to using whenever she walked any distance. She went to Nanny and put her hand on the goat's horn and together they headed down the path towards the washpool. I left Tod where he was and went after them.

'Oma!'

She waved me away but I followed some distance behind. When I arrived at the wash she was sitting at one end, crying. Nanny was standing behind with her head low. I sat down beside her.

'I'm so sorry, Oma.'

'It's not your fault. That's what Shirl needs to understand.'

It was almost dark and the air was getting cold. I could see steam rising from the water.

'It *is* my fault. I played the button-box.'

If Oma was looking old, this news aged her before my eyes. She turned to me and her face was grey.

'What?' she gasped.

'That fellow – the lawyer – he took it but he fell off, or his horse threw him, and he dropped the button-box. I found the bits of it.'

A look of complete bewilderment crossed my grandmother's face. She closed her eyes for a moment and took a deep breath.

'It's not your fault. If anyone's to blame, it's me. Ort would have left that thing lying quietly under the bed.'

She wiped her eyes and sighed. 'I'm going to tell you a story, Ellie, a true story that happened long ago. I don't know everything but I know enough.'

She looked towards Mt Ossa. 'There was once a big settlement here.'

'In the old times,' I said. I knew Spit Farm was a

poor rundown place compared with what it had once been.

'I shouldn't encourage you by mentioning it but you know those tales you used to tell about the Gleam land? Well, this country was like that for a while. Everything flourished.'

Oma picked up a handful of dirt. 'This is hungry ground, El. It was hungry before and it's hungry now but for a while there was a time of plenty, a time when the family bred up big and there were hamlets all over the mountain.'

'Spitville,' I said. 'Bald Hill, Fel's Hollow.'

There was nothing left of those places now but I knew where they had been. When I was little I'd seen a map of them in my mind. I drew it for Tod and taught him the names and I was the one who found the ruins of a kiln at Fel's Hollow. Pop was glad of the bricks. He brought them home and used them to repair the holdfast.

Oma let the dirt run through her fingers. 'How do you think this poor land could support so many people? How could this thin mountain soil and the short growing season feed a big mob like that?'

She fell silent and stared across the pool. The first stars were coming out and I could see them floating on the quiet water.

'It was the button-box,' she said. 'Your pop's grand-mother had it, or maybe it was his great-grandma. Her name was Alma West, and they say she got sick – perhaps she was dying. Who knows what made her think she'd find an answer to her illness on the far side of the country, but that's where she went. She headed towards the Palisades and somewhere out there she found an old woman, a cure-all by the name of Ilk, who fixed her up. The journey saved her life but it took it too, in the end. Because she came back with that button-box.

'Things went well at first. The hens laid double-yolkers. The fruit trees cropped twice a year instead of once, and every cow had twins. They had to build the holdfast to store all the food that grew here. But if the instrument could give, it could also take away, and what it took was harmony. People got greedy, Ellie. They had plenty but they wanted more.

'There were fights. Everyone wanted to play that button-box. Alma had to lock her door at night in case someone came to steal it. In the end she decided it was doing more harm than good. She wanted to get rid of it, but that was easier said than done.'

Oma wasn't making much sense but I kept quiet and listened.

'In those days they had a bonfire on Bald Hill each year to mark the end of winter. When Alma took out the instrument everyone thought she was going to play – and whether it was music she would produce or food or gifts I can't say.'

Nanny Gitto let out a forlorn little cry. She looked as though she was listening, taking in every word.

'The fire had been lit for hours. It was a great blaze. It had all the winter prunings from the new orchards as well as logs and tree stumps, because at that time they were still clearing the land. Alma looked into the flames, then suddenly she threw the instrument into the fire. She wanted that to be the end of it. But the button-box didn't burn and a dozen people rushed in after it. Many were badly hurt and one man died. That was the power it held, Ellie.'

Oma went quiet and I thought she wasn't going to say any more. It was cold and she was shivering. I looked to the rail to see if any washing was hanging there, something I could put around her, but there was nothing except a pair of Uncle Vern's long johns.

'Alma tried to destroy the instrument many times,' Oma continued. 'Nothing worked. She was followed wherever she went. People couldn't take their eyes off that button-box. So she decided to take it back where it came from. She believed it could only be destroyed in the place where it was made and if she could do that, all the harm it had caused would be undone.'

'The Gleam country,' I said. 'It's beyond the Palisades.'

'Ellie, there's no such place.'

I said nothing but I knew that wasn't true.

'It was autumn when she headed over the pass.' Oma bowed her head and hugged herself. 'The days are so hot yet the nights are freezing,' she muttered.

'We should go home,' I suggested. 'Or get into the wash.'

When Oma took off her dress and stepped into the water, I followed. We sat under the chute and took turns letting the hot water gush over our shoulders.

'What happened, Oma?'

'Alma didn't come back. The weather turned and she didn't make it across the pass. Whoever found her — it might have been Ort's mother — took the button-box and hid it away.

'Things went back to normal after that. There were hungry times and times when there was enough, but there was bad feeling in the community and people split up and went their separate ways.'

Nanny began pacing up and down on the bank, looking wistfully over the water. She hated getting wet but she wanted to be near us. Oma kept talking.

'The button-box was never used again and after some time it was forgotten, or almost forgotten. Over the years, descendants of those who had once lived on Mt Ossa came looking, pretending they were visiting or passing through.'

'Is that why everyone came to Pop's funeral?'

'We invited them, Ellie. It was my idea. I wanted everyone to see it buried with Pop. He wanted that too. He didn't want it to be handed down to you or Tod.' She slowly lowered herself under the surface and came up again. 'There, now you know everything.' She seemed relieved.

I began undoing her plaits. I didn't have the carding comb so I used my fingers. Her hair was thin and patchy and strands of it came out in my hand.

There was no sound except for the rushing water.

'I took Lil's necklace,' I told her.

She turned to me and her mouth fell open.

'I needed to pay the tinker man for fixing the button-box.'

'Did he play it?'

'No, I did. The first time Hattie laid an egg and the beans shot up. The next time things didn't go so well.'

'It was the same in the past, Ellie. It's unpredictable. Where have you put it?'

'It's in the shade-cave.'

'So close.' She turned and stared into my eyes. 'This is what you'll do, Ellie. Go and hide that thing deep in the cave, as far back as you can, then block up the entrance. Do it first thing tomorrow.'

'I'll do it now, Oma. I'll go and get the lamp.'

I pulled my clothes back on and ran all the way to the shack. Everyone had gone to bed and I was careful not to make any noise when I took the lamp from its place in the porch.

I met Oma before I reached the wash. Perhaps the bad news I'd told her had affected her; she had her arm over Nanny's back and I could see she was struggling. I put her other arm over my shoulder and took her weight.

'Can you help me home?' she asked.

It was late by the time we got back. Oma's clothes were damp because she hadn't dried herself properly and I tried to help her into her nightdress, but she wouldn't have it.

'Do what I told you, Ellie,' she whispered as she lay down. 'Do it right now and promise me you'll never touch that thing again.'

I turned and ran down the path with every intention of doing exactly as she said, but when I reached the cave I couldn't find the satchel. I shone the lamp inside the entrance but the button-box was gone.

9

Dust Devils

TOD HAD BEEN sleeping in the front room since Pop died and that's where I looked as soon as I got home. He wasn't in bed so I went to the holdfast and called. When there was no answer I walked past the yards to the horse paddock, and that's where I found him. He was sitting on the fence talking to Sol and he waved when he saw me. His face shone in the moonlight.

'It's going to be all right, El,' he said. 'I've fixed everything.'

'What do you mean?'

'I sang and I played. It will all come right by morning.'

As he spoke a warm wind blew up from the west.

'You went to the shade-cave by yourself?'

He nodded.

'Where's the button-box?'

'Back under the bed. It was good to play it, Ellie.

It was cold down there but it warmed me up. My hands are still tingling.' He held them out and stared at them. 'It gave me such a feeling – I can't describe it. And somebody was there – some old fellow, he came to hear the music. Oma'll be better by morning, that's what he said.'

'Where did he come from? What was he like?'

My brother shrugged. 'I couldn't see him in the dark.'

'Tod, you shouldn't have touched that thing!'

I turned and ran to the shack and as I did the breeze grew stronger, raising dust devils in the yard. They twisted past Shirl and Vern's shed and disappeared behind the shack. I went into the front room and reached under the bed. A gourd was knocking hollow against the window. It sounded like someone trying to get in. I pulled out the button-box, then went and hid it in an empty bin in the feed shed. It was too late to go back to the cave that night. I would do it first thing in the morning.

I slipped into bed beside Auntie Lil. Oma was sleeping next to the wall and she was breathing strangely, each intake of air followed by a wheezing sigh. I lay down, listening to her, and after a while I realised Lil was awake and listening too.

'She's taken a turn for the worse, Ellie. I don't know what possessed her to go bathing in the wash at night.'

'Maybe she'll feel better tomorrow.' My voice was tight.

'Let's hope. But don't you fret, girl. Mountain people are tough and your grandma is tougher than most.'

The fact that my aunt said that made me worry more, and it took me a long time to get to sleep. I woke before dawn and the bed was empty. The day was already warm and the wind was rattling the roof stones. Oma and Auntie Lil were in the kitchen and they were speaking in hushed tones.

'If Shirl keeps this up it's going to come out in the end, Lil. She's harping at Vern day and night. She won't let up.'

I opened the door a crack and peeped through. Oma was leaning over the bench and the air was full of dust. She was bent like an old lady.

'Sooner or later he'll give in and tell her and I don't want Ellie hearing anything from Shirley.'

'Don't weary yourself. Go back to bed.' Auntie Lil was plugging a gap in the wall with a flour bag, trying to keep out the dust.

I watched Oma hobble towards the door and I was so shocked by her appearance that I didn't get out of the way. I just stood, staring.

'Oh, you're awake,' she said.

'Oma, what's happened to you?'

'I must have come down with something, going to bed in wet clothes like that.'

She half fell onto our palliasse and I helped her move up so she could lean on the pillows. I looked at her face. Her skin was dry and crisscrossed with a thousand tiny lines. It was like looking at a country that I'd never seen before. She closed her eyes.

'I'm tired, Ellie, too tired to keep secrets. There's

something you should know, something I need to tell you while I can. There's truth in what Shirley says about you not being kin.'

I stared at her in shock.

'Ellie, we reared you – I reared you – so you're as much part of this family as anyone—'

There was a loud twang from the side of the shack.

'A board's sprung loose,' Auntie Lil called. 'I'll go and have a look.'

Oma took my hand. 'It was a hard winter the year you came. Leela caught a hacking cough that she couldn't shake.'

'What are you saying?'

'Leela wasn't your ma. She was carrying a baby but she died before it was born. You arrived just after.'

I couldn't believe my ears. I looked at Oma's face, so grey and drawn. She was sick – that was it. That was why she was talking nonsense.

There was hammering outside.

Oma pulled me close. 'I found you one morning after some herders had passed through. I was out early with the goats. When I heard you cry I thought it was the bleating of a newborn kid.'

'Stop, Oma!' I gasped. 'Stop speaking rubbish. It's not true.'

'You were only a few weeks old. You were lying in the grass not far from the remains of a campfire and you were wrapped in the finest shawl I'd ever seen. Someone had set stones into the ground around you so you wouldn't roll downhill.'

I let go of my grandmother's hand. 'No, Oma. You don't know what you're saying—'

She was talking quickly, as if she wanted to tell me all she could before her breath ran out. She gazed into my face and her eyes had a milky look to them.

'You weren't alone. I don't know what surprised me more, you or Nanny Gitto.'

The hammering stopped and the back door slammed as Auntie Lil came in.

'Another board's split,' she said. 'The timber's so dry and splintery. If this wind keeps up—'

She looked at us and fell silent.

'I don't care how surprised you were!' I cried.

'Don't speak to your grandmother like that,' Lil said.

'She's not my grandmother,' I shouted. 'Which means you're not my aunt either. Why didn't you tell me before?'

I had a pain in my chest and my ears were ringing.

'There was no reason to,' Oma sighed. 'It makes no difference. You're my granddaughter and that's all there is to it.'

'That's not all there is to it. It makes a big difference to me!'

'We expected your people would come back for you—' Oma began.

'My *people*?'

'The herders. Every day we looked towards the pass.' Oma was struggling for breath. It was exhausting her to talk. 'Tell her, Lil.'

'Flo decided if those herders would leave a baby lying on the ground they had no claim on it.'

Oma reached for my hand but I pulled it back. 'One day I saw someone coming and it was all I could do not to run away and hide you. But it wasn't the herders, it was Shirl returning from Scarp. I knew she'd say I shouldn't have rescued you, so to make matters simple, we decided that you'd be Tod's new sister. Shirl knew Leela was pregnant so it made perfect sense. We'd say that she hadn't survived but you had.'

'So everyone knew except Shirl?'

'Not everyone. Tod doesn't know.'

'What don't I know?' Tod said as he came into the kitchen. He put his head inside the door of our room and caught his breath at the sight of Oma.

'What's going on?' he asked.

'I'm leaving, that's what.' I swept past him and out of the shack, banging the back door. I could hear Oma calling after me and the sound of her voice, so weak and frail, made the pain in my chest worse.

'You should have told me!' I yelled over my shoulder.

Tod came running after me. 'Stop, Sis. Wait! What's wrong with Oma?'

I turned to face him. 'She's worse, much worse. Whatever tune you played wasn't a healing song. And I'm not your sister!'

Tod looked totally bewildered. 'What? How can that be?'

'Ask them.' I nodded towards the back door then

went to the feed shed. Tod stood, uncertain for a moment, then headed back inside. Once he was gone I grabbed Pop's hat and the button-box, then went to the barn and got a saddle and bridle, Sol's bridle. There was no point in taking one of our mountain ponies. I had a long way to go and I needed a horse that was fit for the journey.

I quickly saddled Sol and cantered past the yards. The sun was up and I didn't stop until I reached Pop's grave. It was covered with a stand of dead sunflowers and the dry leaves rustled in the wind. Some of the stalks were broken and the big flowerheads faced down, dropping their seeds on the hard ground. I jumped off and picked them up, putting handfuls in my saddlebag. It was all the food I had. Then I spoke to Pop, although he didn't deserve it. He was as bad as Oma and Auntie Lil. How could he have been so dishonest? It wasn't Shirley Serpentine who was full of wild imaginings, it was me, believing I was part of this family. And Shirley was right about the bad luck. Look at the trouble I'd brought.

'I'm going to get rid of the button-box,' I told Pop. 'I'm going to make everything right.' I climbed back on Sol and headed towards the pass, knowing that nothing would ever be right again.

PART TWO

10

The Pass

IT WAS MID-MORNING by the time I reached
the top of Bald Hill. I looked back and saw that Spit
Farm was already tiny in the distance, a cluster of grey
ramshackle sheds clinging to the steep hillside. They
looked rickety and frail, as if a decent wind might blow
them away, and for a moment I imagined it happening.
I could hear that wind in my ears. It wasn't a gentle
breeze, it was an angry roaring gale, the type of wind
that takes everything in its path. I grabbed a handful
of Sol's mane to steady myself. Then I closed my eyes
and tried to calm down. When I opened them the place
I'd called home looked strange to me. Who was I, if
not Leela's daughter, Tod's sister, and Pop and Oma's
granddaughter? How could they have lied all these
years, pretending I was blood when I wasn't? Shirley
Serpentine was right: I didn't belong, not at Spit Farm
and maybe not anywhere in this world.

Some goldwings swooped past, filling the air with their raucous cries. They were winter birds, confused by the season, and I felt they cried for me. I was as confused as they were. The ground had shifted under my feet and nothing was solid anymore.

I took a deep breath and rode on as the cries of the goldwings faded. Soon all I could hear was the sound of Sol's hoofs on the stony track, the buzzing of insects and sound of seedpods cracking in the heat.

There was a way-hut near the pass. I reached it that evening and I was glad nobody else was there. There were no horses outside and the door hung open, banging in the wind.

I pumped water into the trough for Sol and looked out over the range. Something was moving between the trees, probably a skitter goat or a feral pig. I hoped no rogue creatures would cross my path while I was alone up there.

I was starving hungry. I ate the sunflower seeds and thought how only a fool would head off over the pass without supplies. Sol grazed at the side of the hut, pulling tufts of dry grass near the corner post. I unsaddled him and rubbed him down and then I leaned against his shoulder.

'It's you and me now, Sol,' I said.

I took the button-box from the saddlebag and went into the hut, bolting the door behind me. There was nothing much inside, just a fireplace and a sleeping bench. I lay down on Sol's saddle blanket.

I was used to having Oma on one side of me and Lil

on the other, but I told myself I'd get used to sleeping alone. I'd have to. A sob rose in my throat but I quickly swallowed it down. There was no point in crying; I had to be strong. I began to think of the journey ahead, hoping there would be huts along the way – if there were no huts I'd have to sleep out.

I had no idea how far it was to the Palisades or how to get there, but I had a tongue in my head so I would ask. It wasn't such a hard thing, I told myself, to travel across plains to the far side of the country, but when I closed my eyes a flock of doubts came and nested in my chest, and once they were lodged, there was no loosening them. I went to sleep and dreamed I was galloping across a country full of shadows and somebody was on my tail. My heart thumped in my chest, drumming out a rhythm, and whoever was after me seemed to be running in time to the beat of it. They were almost upon me when I woke with a start. Someone was pounding at the door.

There was an unspoken rule in the mountains that the way-huts belonged to everyone. You couldn't get there first and claim a hut as your own. But I wasn't going to open the door. I lay perfectly still in the dark, feeling as if I'd woken from one nightmare into another.

Bang! That wasn't the sound a hand made knocking at the door; it must have been a hammer. There was a scratching noise, then another crash. The whole hut shook with the blow.

I looked around for somewhere to hide. There was only the chimney and it wasn't wide enough to climb inside. Without making a sound I got up and grabbed a lump of wood that was lying on the hearth. I stood with my back to the wall, the door on one side of me and a little window on the other. Everything went quiet except for my heart, which was beating so loudly I was sure whoever was on the other side of the door could hear it. When the door was struck again I almost cried out. I hoped it would hold.

There was silence outside. I leaned forward and peeped out the window. Something white moved in the darkness, backing away. At first I thought it was a man crouching, a man in a white shirt. I heard him grunt. Then I realised it wasn't a man – it was a goat. It was Nanny Gitto! She pawed the ground then lowered her head and charged. Crash! This time the door gave way. It swung open and Nanny was inside.

'Nanny, you gave me a heart attack!'

She stamped her foot and stared at me. Someone had put a collar around her neck and a gunny sack was tied to it. I took off the collar. Inside the sack were half a dozen hoe cakes, along with a hunk of cheese wrapped in oilcloth, a milking mug and small parcel containing a tiny folded shawl. At least, I thought it was tiny but it kept unfolding until I held a length of pale fabric that was bigger than I was. It was light as air and it smelt faintly of milk – sweet, fresh milk. There was a letter with it, and when I unfolded it a handful of coins fell onto the floor. I went outside and read by the light of the moon.

My dearest Ellie,

You came with this shawl and I've kept it all these years. Keep yourself warm.

Your uncle wanted to come straight after you but I've told him to wait. You need time to get used to what you've learned. I'm sorry I didn't tell you sooner. I hope you're not thinking of going to the Trading Post but if you are the coins are for a bed. Lil is writing this letter for me because I am very tired.

All my love,
Oma

I bit my lip to stop the tears, but they welled up anyway and it wasn't long before they overflowed. Sol came and stood next to me and that made me cry harder. I looked back the way I had come. For a moment I wanted nothing more in the world than to saddle Sol and ride straight home. But that was the thing. It wasn't my home; not really, not anymore.

'I can't go back,' I sobbed. 'I can only go forward.'

I was drying my tears when I heard a bump inside the hut. Nanny had dragged the gunny sack from the bench and the hoe cakes were scattered on the floor. She was eating them.

'No, Nanny!' I tried to shoo her out but she wouldn't

have it. She twitched her tail and glanced at me in annoyance as if I was the one causing the trouble. Then she jumped onto the sleeping bench and sat down. I picked up the remains of the cakes and put them in the gunny sack, then climbed up beside her, spreading Oma's shawl over both of us. It was light as a feather but surprisingly warm.

Nanny stretched out. She was a big goat and she didn't leave much room. I lay jammed against the wall but I was glad to have her next to me. I went to sleep to the sound of her chewing her cud.

THE NEXT MORNING I woke to the noise of peas being poured into a bin, or that's what I thought it was until my nose filled with the pungent smell of goat dung. I opened my eyes.

'Nanny, get outside!'

She was standing in front of the fireplace and she gave me a steady look as she finished dropping a load of pellets on the hard-packed floor of the hut. Then she tossed her head and trotted through the open door.

I ate hoe cakes soaked in fresh milk for breakfast, then I slipped the button-box back in the saddlebag and left before dawn, heading towards the pass. Nanny skipped ahead, nibbling dry grass on either side of the track, and Sol settled into a steady trot.

We'd been travelling for a couple of hours when I saw a mule cart coming down the hill towards me.

It was driven by a woman who looked a bit like the tinker's wife. She was worn and dusty and her mouth was set in a grim line. There were three children behind her, hunched down in the cart and staring back the way they came. The oldest boy held a baby. Their goods were half covered with a piece of torn canvas.

The woman wore her hat low over her eyes and she urged the mule on as if she wanted to get past me as fast as she could. Did she take me for a robber?

I thought she was going to pass without a word but when she glanced up at me her face changed and she smiled. The cart lurched to a halt.

'It's all right. It's only a girl,' she called over her shoulder.

The children turned around and three more heads popped up from under the canvas.

'You gave me a fright,' she said. 'It could have been anyone under that hat.'

A small boy in the back pointed to Nanny.

'Mama, look at the horns!'

'And look at that horse!' one of the girls cried.

'Where are you heading?' the lady asked.

'The Trading Post.'

'We've just come from there. Are you trading the goat?'

Nanny trotted over to the cart and nosed one of the little girls. There were squeals of delight. Nanny loved children, especially small ones.

'She's not for sale,' I said. 'I'm staying at the Trading Post on my way to the plains.'

'The plains?' The woman raised her eyebrow. 'Surely you're not travelling that far by yourself.'

'Further. I'm going to the Palisades.'

The woman gave a faint smile and shook her head. 'There's no such place. You mean the Western Ranges. Why are you going there? There's nothing out that way.'

I thought the whole world would know about the Palisades, but I supposed people called places by different names. I said I was visiting relatives.

'The roads are dangerous. You shouldn't be travelling alone. Where's your ma?'

I was about to tell her that I didn't have a mother when it occurred to me that it might no longer be true.

'She's gone on ahead,' I said.

'Well, don't tarry. You'd best catch up with her quick as you can.'

She wished me well and her children waved as the cart creaked along the rutted track.

⟋⟍⟍⟋

THE ROAD NARROWED as it followed the ridge-line and the vegetation on either side grew sparse. There were thorn bushes, thistles and the prickly shrubs Oma called Flo's Curse because of the spines that got caught in the belly fleece of goats and made her swear when she was spinning. Soon there were only clingbells and the tiny mountain stars that could grow anywhere, and then no plants at all, just the bare ground with the sun beating down on it.

I reached the pass at midday and looked down over the plains. A heat haze hung over the country but I could see green grasslands towards the east. The western plains were brown.

When I reached the turn-off to the Trading Post I met people on the road, a couple who'd come from the back country in the east and were heading north with packs on their backs.

'We're looking for work,' the lady said. 'We can't farm in this weather. Our water is drying up and our crops are failing.'

'We thought the drought was in the west but now it's started here as well.' Her husband wiped the sweat from his brow. 'Something's upset the seasons.'

I bowed my head and moved on.

For a while I heard nothing except Sol's hoofs on the stone road. Then there were voices ahead. I came around a corner and met more travellers, half a dozen people heading in the same direction as me. They were loaded up. One man led a packhorse and another pushed a handcart stacked high with bags. They were dusty and tired and the conversation was about the weather.

'There might be rain in the south,' said the man with the horse. 'That's what I'm hoping.'

A lady walked on one side of him, helping an elderly man. 'It's got to change soon. It can't get much worse. How are you travelling, Pa? Do you need to rest?'

'I'll rest when I find that rainman.'

'What's he on about?' the man with the horse asked.

'There's a travelling show up ahead. He's got hopes of finding a weatherman.'

The man with the handcart gave a weary laugh. 'Those rainmakers are fakes. It's just entertainment.'

'If I told him once I've told him a hundred times. But Pa likes to dream.'

'I saw one once,' her father said. 'It was with this same outfit too. I was just a kid at the time but it's something I'll never forget. His name was Pappy Storm.'

'Made it rain, did he?' The man with the cart laughed again.

'Rain, sun, wind and calm. He could do it all. He had it at his fingertips. I saw it with my own eyes. I swear it.'

'Entertainment's welcome, whatever it is,' said the man with the horse. 'How far is it to the Trading Post?'

'We should get there by dark.'

The conversation returned to the drought. They were all worried, except one fellow who walked apart from the others, a frail old man who seemed untroubled by the heat.

'I don't know why everyone's fretting about an early summer,' he muttered. 'There's been dry spells before.'

He wore old-fashioned garb, a ragged frockcoat that hung on his thin frame and a wide hat that was turned up at the back. I wondered how he could wear a coat in the heat but he seemed quite cool. I couldn't see his face for the hat. The brim was wider than his shoulders.

'Where are you heading, girlie?' he asked in a wheezy voice.

It crossed my mind that I probably shouldn't talk to

every stranger I met, and this man was stranger than most. His boots had pointed toes and they were laced up at the side with leather thonging. Unlike everyone else, he was carrying nothing, not even a bag. He fell into step beside Sol and he must have thought I didn't hear him because he asked the same question again. 'Where are you heading?'

When I didn't answer he reached towards Sol's rein and suddenly I bit the dust. I didn't know what had happened: one moment I was riding and the next I was on the ground. There was a searing pain in my side and the man was staring into my face. Then I must have passed out.

When I opened my eyes, there was no sign of the old man. A fellow with orange whiskers was bending over me. 'That's a wild mount!' he exclaimed. Nanny was sniffing my boots, looking concerned. I turned my head and saw Sol on the far side of the road, held by a rough-looking man on a cow pony.

'This horse's too flighty for a kid like you,' he called across. 'Tell her, Jake.'

'Much too wild,' the orange-whiskered man said as he helped me up. 'You could've broken your neck.'

I clutched my side and gasped for breath, realising what had happened. Sol had shied. It was unlike him to behave like that.

'Looks like you've cracked a rib,' the fellow remarked. 'That black horse is way too big for you. It's a long way to fall.'

The other man rode across me, leading Sol. He had

long hair that hung out from under his hat in greasy strands.

'We trade in horses,' he said. 'You need something your own size, not a big mount like this.' He handed me Sol's rein.

'A quiet pony,' his friend suggested. He stepped back and looked me up and down. 'Tell you what, how about we fit you out with a more suitable horse?'

I shook my head. I was dazed from the fall and my side was hurting. I didn't want to talk to these men and I was glad when the fellow with the handcart came and asked if I was all right.

'Come on, Jake. We'll miss the show.' The man with greasy hair started trotting down the road. His friend got on his horse, a rangy chestnut mare who stood waiting with her ears back.

'Be seeing you,' he said.

I hoped not. I waited until they were gone. I didn't like the look of either of them. What that lady said was true – I shouldn't be travelling alone.

11

The Trading Post

IT WAS EVENING by the time I arrived at the Trading
Post. It was a battered old building that stood on the
side of a hill. One of the verandah posts had broken off
so that the roof hung down, covering one front window
like a hat over an eye. Horses were tied to the hitching
rail and a boy sat on the steps watching the road. He
had dark hair tied back in a ponytail and a rope slung
over his shoulder. His shirt had so many patches you
could no longer see the original material. He looked at
Nanny and his eyes widened, then he stared hard at Sol
and gave a long low whistle.

'That's a real nice horse. Is he a local breed?'

I slid to the ground as carefully as I could. There was
a seat next to the hitching rail and I eased myself onto it.
I was bone tired and every part of me was aching. I was
also famished.

I shook my head.

'Is he yours?'

'He belongs to my brother.'

The boy gazed at Sol in admiration. 'I wish I was your brother.'

I held my side and stared at the ground but the boy seemed set on conversation. He pointed to Sol's shoulder. 'Is that a brand? Looks like a moon. I bet he's lucky.'

I glanced at the boy. He wore ragged pants and he was thin as a beanpole.

'If I had a horse like that I'd never let him out of my sight,' he said.

'My thoughts exactly!' came a voice from the verandah. I looked up and saw one of the horse traders leaning over the rail, the man with the whiskers.

Nanny skittered away into some bushes on the other side of the road.

'I've decided to make you an offer, girl,' the man said.

'I'm not interested,' I told him.

He came down the steps and stood in front of me. 'You'd better be.' He put his hand on the back of the seat. 'The truth is I've taken a shine to your mount so I'll do you a good deal, swap him for a cow pony and throw in some cash.'

The boy came and sat beside me on the seat. 'Where's your brother?' he asked.

'Scat,' the fellow said. 'We're talking business.'

The boy ignored him. 'Where's your folk?'

I hadn't wanted to talk to the boy but now I was glad of his company.

'Up ahead,' I said. 'Where's yours?'

He nodded towards the building. 'Round the back. And there's one more to come.'

The horse trader leaned towards me. 'I told you before, that horse is too big for a girl your size.'

I looked the fellow in the eye. 'Get lost.'

If the boy hadn't been sitting beside me I wouldn't have spoken so boldly.

The man put his hands on his hips. 'Now listen here, girly—'

'She said she's not interested, mister.' The kid couldn't have been much older than Tod but he spoke like a grown up.

'Of course she's interested. She knows a good deal when she sees one and so do I.'

'You don't know dung from wild honey!' The boy stood up. He was very tall but he didn't look too strong.

The horse trader pushed him in the chest. 'No cheek from you, boy.'

Just then a man came around the corner of the building. He wore overalls and carried a sledgehammer.

'Luca, stop scrapping and come and help with the tent.'

When the man strode towards us the horse trader walked up the steps and went into the Trading Post. I breathed a sigh of relief.

'Them cowboys think they own the world,' the boy said.

'Come on,' the man called. 'It's set-up time. What are you doing?'

'Meridian told me to wait here.'

'Well, I'm telling you to come and help with the tent.' He turned and walked back the way he'd come. The boy followed and I noticed he was wearing a strange pair of high-soled boots, gum rubber, not leather.

I looked down the road. A pony appeared, pulling a shabby little buggy with writing on the side: DR ELIXIR'S TRAVELLING MEDICINE SHOW – CURE WHAT AILS YOU. It was driven by an old man with a shock of white hair. There was the sound of clinking glass as he pulled up in front of the Trading Post.

The buggy was covered in dust and the paintwork was faded. I could just make out a list of complaints: CRAMPS, COLIC, BAD BLOOD, BRUISES, BRAIN FAG, HEART ACHE, TWISTED BOWEL. The words became smaller towards the end – WARTS, NITS, POOR EYESIGHT and BLINDNESS. The last word was printed in letters that were so tiny I had to walk right up to the buggy to read it.

The old man noticed me and stepped down from the seat. He only had one arm and there was a bottle tucked under his stump.

'What can I do for you, miss? It is *miss*, isn't it?' He lifted my hat and one of my plaits fell out. I put it back and jammed the hat down hard.

'Are you a doctor?'

'Close as you're going to get in these parts. What's the problem?'

'My rib. I think it's—'

'Broken, bruised or strained – this tonic will do the trick. Dr Elixir's Original Extract can cure any affliction.' He held up the bottle.

'How much is it?'

I took out the coins Oma had given me and the doctor glanced over my shoulder. He held out his hand for the money. 'That looks about right,' he said, passing me the medicine.

'Hold it, Stumpy. Don't you dare!'

A woman appeared at the front door of the Trading Post. She had a husky voice and her fluffy blonde hair bounced as she hurried down the steps.

'Since when do you sell to children?' she asked, taking the bottle from me.

A tiny rolled cigarette was stuck to her bottom lip.

'It's all right,' I told her. 'I want the medicine.'

'No you don't, love.' She ran her hand through her hair and I saw she had a ring on every finger. 'Shame on you, Stumpy.' She gave the bottle back to the doctor then looked at me with concern. 'What's your name, girl?'

'Ellie.'

'I'm Meridian.' She had blue eyes and her face was kind. She smelt faintly of cloves. It might have been the cigarette.

'You've come a long way, Ellie, but it's nothing compared with the distance ahead. Where are you going? No, don't answer that – let me tell you.'

She took my hand and I saw she had a tattoo on the inside of her wrist. It was the size of a coin and it looked like a star, but when I peered closer I saw it was a compass rose, pointing north, south, east and west. She turned my hand over and stared at my palm. 'A long journey and a curious one. You have a double life line. Do you dream of yourself elsewhere?'

When I shook my head she felt my fingers, carefully bending each one back. She frowned. 'If your fingers were supple I'd say you're travelling light, but they're stiff. And I only have to look into your eyes to see you're carrying a great burden.'

'Meridian, don't give it away for free,' the old man sighed. 'We earn little enough as it is.'

He climbed back onto the seat and drove the buggy up the lane beside the Trading Post. Meridian kept feeling my fingers. 'Am I right?' she asked.

I nodded. The button-box wasn't very heavy but it was a weight on my mind and on my heart. I found my eyes suddenly filling with tears. She looked at me thoughtfully. 'You're done in, girl. How long have you been on the road?'

'Only two days.' It felt like much longer.

'Are you on foot?'

I pointed to Sol and she gazed at him and scratched her head.

'And you're alone?'

'Except for my animals. I also have a goat.' I called Nanny and she trotted across the road.

'Good heavens!' Meridian drew on her cigarette. She looked at my goat and she looked at me. I could tell she was weighing things up in her mind.

'Have you eaten?' she asked.

I shook my head.

'Come then. Bring your livestock.'

She walked up the lane and I followed with Nanny and Sol.

The buggy was parked behind the Trading Post along with several dilapidated wagons. The doctor was unhitching the pony and the boy was holding a tent peg while the man in overalls knocked it into the hard ground with the sledgehammer. The tent was old and patched and there was a sign in front of it: HANNIBAL GRAND – TEST YOUR STRENGTH AGAINST THE STRONGEST MAN. There was a row of horses tied behind, eating from hay nets.

'Put your mount with ours,' Meridian said. 'Do you want to tie up your goat?'

I shook my head. 'She doesn't like being tied up.'

Nanny ran up to one of the wagons, a lopsided contraption with wooden sides and a canvas roof.

'She's no fool. That's the feed wagon.' Meridian laughed, a deep husky sound.

I unsaddled Sol and tied him with the other horses. Then I took the button-box from my saddlebag and put it in the gunny sack, which I slung over my shoulder. I followed Meridian to a wagon that had 'cook' painted on the side in big faded letters. Meridian was a large lady and the door was narrow. She had to squeeze through sideways.

The wagon had a bench in the middle with a chopping board on one end and a pump stove on the other. Something delicious was bubbling in a pot and the smell of it made my stomach rumble. There were boxes under the bench and Meridian pulled one out and told me to sit down. I put the gunny sack between my feet.

She dished out a bowl of stew and watched with satisfaction as I ate, then she brought out a pink teapot and some pretty china cups.

'This is the good tea set. I use it for the customers. I knew you were coming, Ellie. I saw it in the leaves.' She made some tea and poured us both a cup.

'There are many reasons why a young girl can find herself travelling alone. I'm not going to ask your business.'

'It's all right. You can ask.' I wanted to tell her everything but I didn't know where to start.

'Has something bad happened?' she asked.

I nodded and the words tumbled out. 'I did a bad thing. I caused a drought and I made my oma sick. She's probably going to die...' My chest hurt when I said that, and it wasn't my bruised rib. It hurt deep inside. 'And she's not even my oma. She should have told me!'

'Told you what?'

'That I wasn't part of the family.'

'I'm not sure I'm following you.' Meridian blew over her tea then sipped it quietly. She seemed about to say something when there was a bang on the side of the wagon.

'Any grub left, Mer?' The doctor appeared at the door.

'Help yourself, Stumpy. The others have already eaten.' She turned back to me. 'I think we need to go to the way-wagon, Ellie. Bring your tea.'

12

The Way-lady

MERIDIAN LED ME along the line of wagons and when we reached Sol she suggested I put my gear in the feed wagon out of the way. Nanny was standing outside it and as soon as Meridian opened the tailgate she jumped straight in. I tried to get her out but she wouldn't budge, and this made Meridian laugh again.

'It's all right. She can help herself to the hay. Just don't let her get into the sacks.'

Meridian put my saddle and saddlebags in the wagon. 'What about your bag?' she asked, looking at the gunny sack.

'I'll keep it with me.'

I followed Meridian to a wagon at the end of the line. It was more faded than the others. It seemed to be covered with a pattern of dots, stars and wavy lines, but when I got close I saw it was a map, or the tracings of one. A sign on the door said THREE-WAYS – LAST OF THE

WAY-LADIES, with the name 'Three-Ways' crossed out and 'Madam Meridian' written above it. There were more words below: DIRECTIONS. ADVICE. KNOW YOUR PAST, DECIDE YOUR FUTURE.

She opened the door and the same map was painted on the inside of it, bright and clear where it hadn't been exposed to the weather. There were roads and rivers and a complicated network of dotted lines that must have been paths or creeks. Every crossing point was marked with a star.

Meridian wore dusty satin slippers and she took them off before she went inside. Her feet were small compared with the rest of her and her toenails were painted sky blue.

'Come in, Ellie.'

A cow's skull was nailed next to the door. It had a dressing gown hanging off one horn and a washcloth off the other. A stove and a kettle sat on a low cupboard on the other side and the walls were pasted over with old handbills and show posters. There were so many faded and curled photos pinned on top that it looked like a bunch of leaves had blown against the wood and stuck there. She pulled one off and handed it to me. It was a picture of an old lady standing at some crossroads. She was leaning on a stick and her smiling face was covered in wrinkles.

'I was about your age when I joined the medicine show. I don't know what would have happened to me if Three-Ways hadn't come along.'

I stared at the picture.

'She was called Three-Ways because she could see the past, present and future. This was her wagon. She taught me everything I know.'

A pair of moth-eaten blinds hung over the window and there was a delicate little fold-up table leaning against the wall between two chairs. I could see a bunk covered with a patchwork quilt behind a curtain that was pulled halfway across the wagon. Clothes hung under it.

Meridian sat down, waiting for me to speak.

I took out the button-box and put it on my lap.

'This is the cause of it all,' I told her.

I knew it didn't look anything special, just some patched-up groan-box that had seen better days.

Meridian rubbed her chin thoughtfully. 'Sometimes I wish Three-Ways was still around. She'd probably know just by looking at it.'

'Know what?'

'The story.'

I was about to explain when she raised her hand. She drank her tea, swirled the leaves and upended the cup on the saucer, asking me to do likewise.

'I can tell you one thing,' she said as she peered into my cup. 'The drought's not your fault. I don't know what caused it, but it wasn't you. It began in the west years ago. That's the big drought I'm talking about, not this one in the mountains.'

'I caused this one,' I said. 'It started on our farm.'

She turned the cup around and peered closer. 'It's spreading,' she said, and then she looked at me and scratched her brow.

'This is serious. Not just for you but for all of us.' She put down the cup. 'I need to do a proper reading. I'll make a map.'

'What sort of map?'

'For you, I'll do a dust map. There are other sorts – star charts, sketch maps and finding trails. Anything that shows the way.'

Meridian set up the table, placing a sheet of paper on it and smoothing it flat. The paper was old and it crinkled under her hands. She leaned over and breathed on it, working carefully from the centre out until the wrinkles were gone.

I noticed how still it was inside the wagon. There was an air of quiet and calm.

'Have you brought your own dirt?' she asked.

'What do you mean?'

'Dust. Earth. A bit of dirt from home. I need to know where you've come from before I can tell where you're going. Some people carry a handful with them wherever they go.'

She pointed to a tiny parcel on the windowsill, wrapped in cloth and tied up with cotton. 'That's my husband Rye's. I don't have one because I've always been on the move.'

I didn't have anything like that, but I turned down the cuff of my shirt and a little pile of dust fell out on the paper. Whether it was from Spit Farm or just dirt

I'd picked up along the way I wasn't sure. There were a couple of grass seeds in it and a thread from my shirt.

'That'll do.' She gently shook the table, distributing the dirt so that it covered the paper in a fine layer. 'Now place your hand underneath, palm up.'

I put my hand under the table and to my surprise, the dust began to move. It drifted to the edges of the paper and I wondered if there was a draught in the wagon. I couldn't feel one.

'You're helping me,' she said. 'Have you done this before?'

'No. Never.'

The dust then drifted towards my hand, moving like iron filings to a magnet. It outlined every finger and made a sort of halo. I looked at the ghost of my hand.

'There's your country,' she said. 'Now let's see where you're heading.'

She tapped the side of the table with her little finger and the dust began to move again, forming lines and ridges. I wondered if it was copying the lines on my palm and I had a look at my free hand, the one that wasn't under the table. There was a long line from my wrist that reached almost to my pointing finger and the dust was making something similar on the paper.

'The Trunk Road,' Meridian said. 'It goes across the plains.'

I watched the dirt from my sleeve form two parallel lines.

'There's that double life again. Do you have a twin?'

'I don't think so.'

She watched the dust gather in piles at one end of the map. It looked like a tiny range of mountains.

'The Palisades.' She raised her eyebrows. 'I didn't know they still existed.'

'You're right,' I said. 'That's where I'm heading.' I stared at the paper before me. The mountains were getting higher.

'How do you do it?' I asked.

'It's hard to explain. You let your mind rest and allow the map to make itself. Once the map's in place I invite people to ask me questions. I'm not always right but I try my best to answer them.'

There was a knock at the door. 'You set, Meridian?' It was the man in the overalls. He poked his head inside. 'Whoops, sorry. Didn't realise you had a customer.'

'Ellie, this is Rye,' Meridian said.

The man reached into the wagon and shook my hand. His face was deeply lined and he looked old, but his eyes were bright and shining.

'We can finish the map later,' Meridian told me. 'Will you come back?'

I nodded and stood up, thanking her for the dinner.

I could tell Meridian was wise. I only had to look at her to know that. Maybe I could ask her things. There was so much I needed to find out. A row of questions lined up in my mind: If I got to the Palisades, where should I go? How could I destroy the button-box and, if I did, would Oma be cured? And if Oma and the others weren't my family, then who was?

'Are you all right, Ellie?' Meridian had opened the

door so I could leave and I realised I was standing in the doorway.

Someone began shouting outside and as I stepped down from the way-wagon I saw it was the boy with the ponytail. A makeshift stage had been set up in front of the buggy and he was standing on it, twirling a rope.

'Ladies and gentlemen, wayfarers and wanderers, welcome to Dr Elixir's Travelling Medicine Show, the greatest little outfit this side of Brink!'

He yelled as if he was addressing a vast crowd and not just the few people who were wandering from the back door of the Trading Post. 'The doctor will be with you shortly. Meanwhile here's a dose of the best fancy roping you'll ever see.'

He put one hand on his hip and spun the rope above his head, looking towards Rye. 'What'll it be – the flat loop, the figure of eight, the side-winding twister?'

'Figure of eight,' Rye called.

The boy flicked his wrist and the rope became a living thing. It floated around him and gathered speed. He changed hands and leapt in and out of the loop, which moved so fast it was a white blur.

'Good, isn't he?' Meridian sounded proud.

'Is he your son?'

'Nephew.'

The crowd applauded and more people gathered.

'Where are you staying, Ellie?' Meridian asked.

'At the Trading Post, if I can get a room.'

'They don't have rooms. They just have a bunkhouse.

I think it'd be best if you stayed with us. You can sleep in the feed wagon if you don't mind sharing with your goat.'

Just then a worried-looking woman with a string bag and a battered suitcase came to the door.

'Are you the way-lady?' she asked.

'Come in,' Meridian said. 'Know your past. Decide your future.'

13

The Travelling Medicine Show

I PUT THE BUTTON-BOX back in my gunny sack and headed to the feed wagon, watching the boy as I went. One moment he was squatting on his hams and the next he was jumping high in the air. The crowd was small but keen. People cheered loudly. I wouldn't have minded staying to see his whole act but I needed to check on Nanny.

A string of lanterns was tied in front of the buggy and Stumpy, the doctor, was opening what looked to be a window at the side. It folded down to form a counter. Behind it were shelves full of bottles. A small woman covered in tattoos came out of the tent and set up a table. She smiled as I passed.

Nanny glanced at me as I climbed into the feed wagon, her mouth full of hay. I took the milking mug from my saddlebag and was kneeling beside her when Rye came and handed me a blanket and a pillow.

'Meridian's worried about you,' he said. 'We're heading to Holman's Flat. If you want you can travel with us.' He scratched Nanny behind the ears and watched the rope-boy.

'And now for the vertical loop spin!' the boy yelled.

Rye went off and a few minutes later I saw him walking up and down with a tray in front of him.

'Charms,' he called. 'Cheap charms. True charms. Charms for all occasions. Carved and painted.'

Nobody took much notice. All eyes were on the boy. He'd lassoed someone, a man whose jaw dropped open in surprise. Everybody laughed as he pulled the man in, looping the rope over his shoulder. He shook the fellow's hand then gave a bow. The audience applauded but when the boy held out his hat only a couple of people threw in coins.

The boy pointed to the buggy and Stumpy stepped forward, holding a mouth trumpet. 'Cure what ails you,' he yelled. 'One drop of Dr Elixir's Original Extract is all it takes.'

The rope-boy came and leaned on the tailgate of the feed wagon.

'They give me a pain,' he said. 'They enjoy the entertainment but they don't want to pay. What's your name, mountain girl?'

'How do you know I'm from the mountains?'

'You've got that moonie look about you.'

'What's that supposed to mean?'

The boy flicked his rope and frowned at the crowd.

'If they were on their last legs they wouldn't cough up and buy the elixir. We're already skint. In a few weeks we'll be broke. What did you say your name was?'

'Ellie West.'

'I'm Luca. You staying with us?'

'I'm staying tonight.'

'That's Meridian, always collecting strays.'

'I'm not stray.'

Stumpy was starting some sort of demonstration, holding up a bottle and a glass bowl.

'Friends and countrymen,' he yelled. 'You're about to witness a miracle. Can I have a volunteer?'

A man standing in front of the buggy put up his hand.

'Let the show begin!' Stumpy cried.

I decided to go and watch and was just stepping down from the wagon when I heard something rip behind me.

'Nanny! Bad goat!'

She was standing on top of the feed sacks and one of her horns had gone through the canvas cover of the wagon. She jumped to the floor, knocking the sack over, and grain went everywhere. Luca gave a hoot.

'Can't you control your goat?'

I shooed Nanny away and pulled the sack upright, then used Pop's hat to scoop up the grain. Luca didn't offer to help. He sat on the tailgate, his long legs dangling.

I had almost finished cleaning up when I heard a click.

'What's this, mountain girl?'

I turned in alarm. Luca had the button-box out of the gunny sack.

'Don't,' I cried. 'Put that down!'

'Steady on, I'm just having a look.' He unhooked the catch and gasped as the bellows swung open. 'What the—'

'Close it!' I yelled, but it was too late. The buttons were moving under his fingers.

Luca's eyes grew wide. He stared at his hands in bewilderment and when I threw myself onto the instrument and reefed it from his grasp he looked amazed. I slipped the catch and put it in the gunny sack.

'Don't you ever touch that again!'

'But it's just a busted squeezebox. It doesn't even work.'

There were cheers and laughter from the audience.

'All symptoms will be gone by morning,' Stumpy cried. 'The extract comes with a lifetime guarantee!'

Luca jumped down from the tailgate and went to the buggy, taking the mouth trumpet from Stumpy.

'Step right up,' he shouted. 'Don't gamble with your precious health.'

A big group of people came up the lane. I wondered where they'd appeared from. As far as I knew there weren't any towns around here. They must have been inside the Trading Post.

Stumpy looked surprised to see the new arrivals. He took back the mouth trumpet.

'Stiff joints, wrenched hams, gout, baldness and twisted cords. One drop is all it takes!'

The audience pressed in and he held up a bottle. It was then that I noticed someone standing at the back of the crowd, the old man with the big hat who'd frightened Sol earlier in the day. He didn't seem so old now. He wasn't looking at Stumpy or the bottle of tonic that he waved in the air. He stared over the heads of the audience and his gaze was fixed on me.

14

The Man with No Dust

THE MAN WEAVED HIS way through the crowd, heading for the feed wagon. He gave me a wave as if we were old friends. That fellow had given Sol a scare and he'd frightened me as well. I didn't want to talk to him, but in no time he was standing at the back of the wagon.

'I think we're heading in the same direction,' he said, tipping his hat. 'Are you going to the Palisades?'

I didn't answer. How could he know where I was going?

'It's not far once you set you mind to it. But you need to know the way. That's where I can help.'

He spoke with his head down, staring at the gunny sack.

'You're mistaken. I'm going to Holman's Flat to visit my cousin.'

I pulled up the tailgate and was glad when some people came and leaned against it.

'Money well spent,' somebody said. 'A drop of that medicine will do us the world of good.'

'Do you want a bottle, Ernie?'

There was a jingling of coins. I peered through a crack in the tailgate but I couldn't see much.

'No sign of your rainman, Pa?'

'More's the pity.'

I recognised the voices of the people I'd met on the road.

'It's a gift. That's what he told me.' The old fellow sounded wistful. 'It's handed from father to son.'

'He would have said that, Pa. It's part of the act.'

'No. It's true. But maybe he didn't have any sons. No sign of any weathermen around here.'

'Let's get a bottle of that elixir before they all go,' somebody said.

The people on the other side of the tailgate dispersed, leaving the fellow in the hat standing by himself. He was still looking right at me and the way he stared made me wonder if he could see through the boards. I kept very quiet and still. After what seemed like an age he shrugged his shoulders and walked away. As soon as he was gone I grabbed my gunny sack and jumped out, running back to the way-wagon.

The lady with the string bag was leaving, looking

much happier than when she'd arrived. I stepped inside and shut the door behind me.

'What is it, child?' Meridian asked. 'Is someone bothering you?' She lifted the blind and peered through the window.

I stood beside her and pressed my face against the glass. The man was gone. The crowd in front of the buggy had grown but I couldn't see him among them.

Someone knocked at the door and I started, pulling away from the window.

'It's all right. It's just a customer.' Meridian squeezed my hand. 'I think you'd better stay here with me. Why don't you have a rest on the bunk?'

I lay down and she pulled the curtain across.

I spent the rest of the evening in the way-wagon. Meridian looked at people's hands, read tea leaves and made maps, giving helpful advice. Most people were travellers who had left home because of the drought, and they wanted to know what to do and where to go. Meridian answered their questions. I listened for a while, then I must have dozed off to sleep. When I woke it sounded like a big crowd had gathered outside.

'Another satisfied customer!' Stumpy was yelling. 'It's a decision you won't regret!' There were cheers and applause.

'And where did you hear of it?' Meridian asked.

I peered through a hole in the curtain and saw a man who had some rope halters slung over his arm. His pack was sitting by the door.

'A fellow from the plains told me. It'll be the biggest

cattle fair there's ever been, at a place called Stolt. Because of the drought all the herders are bringing their stock to market and the prices will be so low that even someone like me can afford a couple of cows to start a herd. But there's no point in going if it doesn't rain. Without rain there'll be no grass to feed them.'

'So that's your question – will it rain?'

'That's the crux of it.'

When the man took off his hat enough dust fell out of his hair to cover the paper on Meridian's table. It made him sneeze and a fine spray covered the paper.

'There's your answer!' she declared. 'It'll rain for sure!'

The man put a coin on the table and left happy.

Meridian turned around and pulled aside the curtain.

'An unusually busy night,' she said. 'I haven't had one like this for a long time.'

'Where's Stolt?' I asked.

'At the end of the Trunk Road. It's the final town before the Western Ranges.'

There was a knock at the door.

'Let's hope this is the last customer.' Meridian stood up and yawned. She closed the curtain and I heard her open the door.

'What can I do for you?' she asked. 'Do you need directions?'

There was no answer.

'A map, perhaps, or would you like advice?'

When the customer didn't reply, Meridian's voice grew sharp.

'What do you want?'

'I want what's mine.'

I drew in my breath. It was *him*, the man in the hat. I recognised his voice.

Very carefully I sat up and looked through the hole. The fellow folded his arms and stared across the table. I saw he had one strange eye – it seemed to have a cloud in it.

'Where are you from?' Meridian asked, puzzled.

'You're the way-lady. You ought to know.'

She looked the fellow up and down. 'Give me some dirt and I'll make you a map.'

The man didn't move. His strange eye began to wander. It took in the wall of pictures, stopping at a photo of Luca. He was posing with a rope over his shoulder. The fellow leaned forward and stared at it.

'I saw that boy outside,' he said.

Meridian took a clean piece of paper and smoothed it on her table.

'Turn down your cuff.'

Still looking at the photo, the man did as she asked, but no dust fell out.

'Perhaps from your hat,' she suggested.

The fellow took off his hat and shook it, but again there was no dust.

'I'll have to read the leaves. I'll make tea.' Meridian stood up and put the kettle on, her back to the table.

'A hat with a brim that big should carry a mountain of dust,' she said. 'How long have you been on the road?'

'It feels like centuries.' The man didn't turn to speak

to Meridian. His eyes roamed around the wagon and came to rest on the curtain. His cloudy eye had a far-away look – it might have been gazing through to the next world – but his right eye was cold and hard and it was staring straight at me. My heart lurched.

'You must be some sort of player,' Meridian said, 'dressed like that. Are you an actor?'

He gave a dry laugh, his eye still fixed on me.

'I guess you could call me a stand-in,' he said.

Meridian frowned as she made the tea. 'That's double talk. Who are you?'

The man didn't reply. He took a deep breath and leaned back on his chair, as if he was considering her question. I wanted to look away but he held me with his gaze. He began whistling a tune.

Meridian took a sidelong look at the man. She poured the tea and put the cup and saucer on the table but he didn't pick it up. I was relieved when he looked back at the pictures.

'This medicine show is a poor outfit compared with what it once was,' he remarked, looking at another photo on the wall. 'Acrobats, exhibits, a snake man and – look at this – a tent as big as a barn.'

'Everything changes,' Meridian muttered. 'Drink your tea.'

The man didn't move.

'You don't drink tea?' she asked.

'I don't drink anything.'

'Well, I'll drink it for you.' Meridian was annoyed now. She drank the tea in silence.

'Do you want to know the past or the future?' she snapped.

'You decide.'

'Swirl the leaves and upend the cup.'

Meridian pushed the cup and saucer across the table but he didn't do as she asked.

'Another time.' He stood up and turned to go.

'Who *are* you?' she asked again.

The man didn't answer. He looked over his shoulder and winked at me and then he left without paying. As soon as he was out the door Meridian reached into her pocket and took out a tattered pack of cards.

I jumped down from the bunk.

She shuffled the pack and drew one, putting it face down on the table. 'I don't have to see it to know that man's dangerous,' she said. 'Turn it over.'

It was a picture of two people joined at the feet. I turned it one way and then the other.

'The twins,' Meridian said. 'A man and his reflection. A man and his shadow. There's no way of telling which is which.'

'What does it mean?'

She frowned and shook her head. 'I've done thousands of readings over the years but I've never come across anyone like that.'

I looked at the photos he'd been staring at – Luca with his rope and the medicine show in the old days. An old fellow with an umbrella was standing at the entrance of a tent. He looked a bit familiar.

'Who's that?' I asked.

'Rye's pa. His name was Pappy Storm.'

'The rainmaker?'

Meridian looked surprised. 'How did you know?'

'People were talking about him.'

Meridian frowned. 'They must have long memories.'

She took the photo down and put it in the cupboard, then she lifted the blind and peered out. 'Let's hope that fellow goes back to wherever he came from.'

There was a big crowd outside now and people were queued up at the buggy window. It was as if they'd appeared from nowhere. The lady with the tattoos had a mob outside her tent and Luca was doing his rope tricks again, his hat on the ground in front of him. People were cheering and throwing in coins.

The old man walked past them. He strode beyond the light of the lanterns and disappeared into the night.

15

The Sidling

PEOPLE WERE LINED UP outside the way-wagon. Meridian was shocked to see so many.

'Looks like our fortunes have changed,' she said, shaking her head. 'Maybe you brought us luck, Ellie.'

That's not what I usually bring, I thought.

'Are you all right to go back to the feed wagon now?'

I said goodnight to Meridian and went to check on Sol, pushing my way through the crowds. I kept an eye out for the man but there was no sign of him. I didn't have to be a way-lady to know he wasn't to be trusted.

'He's just some weird fellow,' I told Sol, putting my arm over his withers and breathing in his smell.

Sol turned his head and put his soft muzzle against my neck. His breath was warm in my ear.

'Thank you, Sol,' I whispered. Hugging that big horse calmed me.

I rubbed my sore ribs and headed to the feed wagon. The tailgate was closed and Rye was standing nearby, selling charms.

'We've never had such a night,' he said. 'Not even in the big towns on the plains. Goodnight, Ellie.'

I climbed inside the wagon and lay down beside Nanny. Despite the noise of the crowds I was asleep as soon as my head hit the pillow.

※

WHEN I WOKE I thought it was morning. The wagon was rocking from side to side and bright light shone through the canvas roof. I looked over the tailgate and was surprised to find it was only the moon. Sol was walking along behind and beyond him I could see the way-wagon, with Meridian in the driver's seat. The road was steep and she was leaning back on the brake. Her horse threw long shadows in the moonlight. She saw me and waved.

'Whoa up!' she yelled.

The feed wagon lurched to a halt and Meridian stopped behind it.

'Where are we?' I asked as she stepped down from the seat. The road was narrow and it wound down the mountain. I could see the other wagons ahead.

'We're going down the Sidling Road. We're halfway to Scarp.'

I looked over the edge of the road. The flatlands were laid out far below like a patchwork bedspread.

There were wriggly lines of rivers and dark areas that could have been forests or crater lakes.

Luca appeared from the front of the feed wagon. He must have been driving it.

'We might as well wait here for Stumpy.'

He let out a shrill whistle and the wagons ahead came to a halt. The night was still, apart from the sounds of the horses chomping their bits and stamping.

Soon we heard singing behind us, some drunken melody:

'*...and though the road is lonesome,*
and though the trail is long,
I'm heading for tomorrow and my heart is full of song...'

Rye walked up the road and joined Meridian.

'Look like the boss's had a good night,' he said.

'Drunk as a skunk.' Meridian folded her arms.

'Seeing is believing!' Stumpy cried as he came into view. 'I'd give my right arm for another night like that.'

'There'll be plenty,' Luca said. 'What's the takings, Stump?'

Meridian looked at her nephew in surprise. 'You've never asked about the takings before,' she said.

'Glad the boy's taking an interest!' Stumpy took a swig from his bottle. He swayed on the seat. 'We go for weeks and hardly sell a thing, then four dozen in one night!' He drained the bottle and threw it over the side of the road.

'I'm almost out of stock. I'll have to make up a new batch.' Laughing, he reached under the seat and dragged out another bottle, pulling the cork with his teeth.

'What are the takings?' Luca asked again, as the buggy pulled up alongside the way-wagon.

'Half a bag of potatoes, a pound of beans and this.' Stumpy tossed Luca a moneybag. 'Count it later, boy. Best to get some distance between Dr Elixir and his patients before morning.' He tried to tap his nose with his finger but missed, and thought this was a great joke.

Luca opened the bag and scooped up a handful of coins. 'Don't accept food next time, Stumpy. Cash is better. That goes for you too, Meridian. And for everyone.'

He looked around. The woman with the tattoos was walking up the road beside an enormous bald-headed man.

'May, Hannibal, do you hear?'

They looked at him blankly.

'Cash only. Is that clear?'

'What's got into you?' Meridian asked.

Luca closed the sack and tied it up with string. 'This tinpot show has turned a corner. I can feel it. How about we hitch that horse of yours to a wagon?' he said to me. 'He's wasted at the moment. Everyone in this outfit has to pull their weight.'

'Luca!'

'It's all right, Meridian. Sol wouldn't mind helping,' I said. 'He's pulled a cart at home.'

'He can help Rusty with the feed wagon. Bring him round the front and we'll harness him.' Luca walked off and Meridian and Rye looked at each other, dumbfounded.

'What's up with him?' Hannibal asked.

'Beats me,' said Rye.

Meridian looked worried. 'Something's amiss.'

I untied Sol and followed Luca. He took a collar and girth out of one of the other wagons.

'Soon we'll buy an extra horse,' he said as he put the collar over Sol's head. 'Do up the side straps, will you?' A lock of hair fell over his eyes and he flicked it out of the way.

'Move aside, Rusty.' He backed Sol into the shafts beside the other horse.

I opened the tailgate and was about to get in when Luca was suddenly behind me.

'Where's that thing? Can I have another look at it?'

'What thing?'

'That busted button-box – where is it?'

'Ellie, would you like to travel with me?' Meridian asked.

'No, she wouldn't,' Luca replied. 'She can stay in the feed wagon.'

'You can't tell me what to do.' I took the blanket and my saddlebags, went to the way-wagon and climbed up on the seat.

Meridian spoke to Luca in a low voice and he kicked the ground with those strange boots of his.

'You've got no ambition, that's your trouble,' I heard him say, then he hopped on the wagon and drove off.

'I'm sorry, Ellie. He's never behaved like this before,' Meridian said as she sat beside me.

'It's all right. It's not your fault, it's the button-box. It makes things happen.' I put the gunny sack on my lap.

'How can that be?' Meridian clicked her tongue and the horse clip-clopped down the road.

'It's got some sort of power. When my pop played, it brought on the spring and made my oma young, but then it did the opposite: it caused the drought and Oma got old and sick.' My throat went tight when I said that. 'Sometimes it makes good things happen,' I whispered, 'but mostly they're bad. I'm getting rid of it. That's why I'm going to the Palisades.'

Meridian was quiet. Bits of Stumpy's song drifted on the night air, '...*take me for my word...true to you my darling...*'

'I think you'd better start at the beginning,' Meridian said. 'Get it off your chest.'

As we travelled down the Sidling Road I told Meridian everything that had happened, from the day Pop died to the time I left Spit Farm. I told her how Oma had told me I wasn't kin, just like my Auntie Shirl had always said, and how Shirl believed I was bad luck. I told her what my grandmother had said about Alma West and the button-box.

Oma always said talking about a trouble made you feel better, but when I reached the end of my story I felt worse, much worse. I wiped my eyes with the back of my hand and tried to hide my tears. Meridian passed me a handkerchief, then asked me to take the reins while she rolled one of her cigarettes.

The road had flattened out and there were trees on either side. The wagon moved in and out of shadow.

'I've heard a lot of people's problems,' she said. 'But this has to be one of the rarest.'

'If I take the button-box to the Palisades, that'll be the end of it,' I told her.

'It might and it might not.' She blew clove-scented smoke into the clear night air and shook her head. 'I don't like to think of you travelling alone. It's much too far. There's all sorts of people on the road.'

I remembered the fellow in the hat and gulped. Meridian must have known what I was thinking. 'Do you have any idea who that man is?'

'Maybe he's the one Tod saw when he played the button-box.'

'He's connected to you in some way. When he first came into the way-wagon I thought he might be a relation.'

A relation! I shuddered at the thought. 'Why do you say that?'

'Just a feeling. But I'm often wrong. I wish I was a better way-lady than I am.'

The trees ended and the road grew steep again. Meridian took back the reins. The wagon rocked from side to side and I looked down over the plains. I could see lights twinkling here and there as if stars had fallen to earth and were signalling to the skies above. The flatlands were vast and I wondered how long it would take me to reach my destination.

'What did you mean when you said that you didn't know the Palisades still existed?'

'I hadn't heard of them in years. It's changeable

country out that way. That's what Three-Ways used to say. It's full of crossing paths and back tracks. I never advise people to go there, not that anyone would, unless they're on a path already. Of course, in the old days people used to go back and forth across those mountains all the time. But that was ages ago.'

'Do you think it will take a long time to get there?'

'For some it could take a lifetime, for others not long at all.'

'Do you think it would take *me* long?' I was thinking about Oma and wondering how long her strength would last.

'I'm not sure.' Meridian was quiet for a while and then she asked what my oma thought about me leaving home.

'She doesn't know.'

'Oh Ellie, she'll be out of her mind with worry.'

'Well, she shouldn't have lied to me!'

Meridian put her hand on my arm and gave it a gentle squeeze.

'I'm not even her granddaughter. Why would she care?'

'You don't mean that, Ellie.'

'I do mean it.' I blew my nose and looked at the gunny sack. 'It's the fault of the button-box. I've a good mind to chuck it over the edge.'

'If it was so easy your great-grandmother would have done the same.'

'She's no relation to me either,' I cried. 'I want to find my real family.' I turned to Meridian. 'Can you help me?'

'People have asked me that before. Sometimes they don't like what they find.'

'I'll like my real family. I'm sure I will.'

Meridian sighed. She reached over and took the gunny sack off my lap, putting it under the seat.

The night was cold. She wrapped the blanket around my shoulders and fixed it with a pin. Then she put her arm around me.

'Is this what Three-Ways used to do?' I said.

'Why do you ask?'

'I don't know.'

I was getting sleepy. I leaned against her as the wagon creaked down the road and before long I felt myself dozing.

'There's something about you, Ellie. You seem older than your years. Have you any interest in the way?'

'What way?' I murmured.

'The mapping and the telling, my line of work.'

'I've always worked on the farm.'

16

Scary

I SLEPT LONG and deep and when I woke I had no idea where I was. My gunny sack was at my feet and I was covered by a blanket. I looked up at a torn canvas roof, trying to remember the night before.

'You fell asleep, my dear, and she put you back to bed. You're in the feed wagon.'

I sat up with a start and looked around. Meridian's blanket was over me and my saddlebags were by my side. Nanny was lying next to me. Her head swayed with the movement of the wagon. She began nibbling one of my plaits.

'Still got a way to go.'

I jumped to my feet and looked behind the grain bags but nobody was there. Sheaves of hay were piled at the front of the wagon.

'Who's there? Where are you?' I asked.

When there was no reply I began riffling through the hay, grabbing armfuls and hurling it into the air. Nanny didn't seem disturbed by whoever was in the wagon with us, but I was. 'Show yourself!' I cried.

'Sit down, Ellie.'

It was a woman's voice, an old woman. And she knew my name.

'Don't be afraid. It's only me. You've known me all your life.'

There was nobody hiding in the hay.

'Don't fuss, my girl,' the lady said.

I shook my head and pinched myself on the thigh. There didn't appear to be anyone in the wagon except me and Nanny Gitto.

'It can't be,' I said under my breath.

There came a nickering laugh. It almost sounded like a bleat.

'Settle yourself. You might as well get some more sleep. It's just on dawn and they won't be stopping for a while.'

I sat down and closed my eyes, thinking hard.

'Nanny, tell me you're not talking,' I whispered.

'All right, I'm not.' She shook her head and her wattles flapped from side to side. I stared at her in the half light and she blinked and stared back.

'If you're not going back to sleep you might as well milk me,' she said. 'I'm feeling rather uncomfortable. Your oma always milked me regularly every morning but you're all over the place. Get the mug out.'

My mind was jumping about like a jackrabbit. I took

a deep breath and asked myself what Oma would do in this situation. She wouldn't panic. She'd tell herself that her mind was playing tricks and then she would calmly get out of the wagon. But I wasn't Oma.

'Stop!' I screamed. 'Stop the wagon!'

When the wagon came to a halt I opened the tailgate and jumped out. Nanny jumped out too. Luca came around the back.

'What's the trouble?'

'There's someone in there.'

He looked behind the sacks as I had done, then he scratched his head and turned to me.

'What are you playing at?'

Meridian stopped behind us. 'What's happened? Bad dream, Ellie?'

I rubbed my eyes. Perhaps that's what it was.

Luca told me to get back in and Meridian asked if I'd rather ride with her.

'What's the hold-up?' Stumpy called.

Nanny jumped back inside, glancing at me over her shoulder.

'Yes, maybe it was a dream,' I told Meridian.

I got back in the feed wagon with Nanny.

'Where's your milking mug?' She didn't move her mouth when she spoke but I heard her voice inside my head clear as day. 'I can't wait all morning, Ellie.'

I stared at my goat for a long moment. Then, in a daze I got out the mug and began milking. The wagon rolled on down the road.

'Did I ever tell you about the goats,' Nanny asked,

'the magnificent goats with horns like mine?'

I hardly had a voice, but I answered, 'I don't know. I thought I made that up.'

'Their horns grew one circle every ten years. Did you know that?'

I didn't respond. I didn't want to encourage her.

'Did you know that?' she demanded. 'Remember your manners, Ellie. When someone speaks it's polite to answer.'

'I guess I knew,' I whispered.

'And what marvellous milk they produced! If you drank it every day it would make you wise and the curd made from the milk could cure any illness.'

'Nanny, why are you speaking?'

'I could ask you the same thing,' she snapped. Then she became thoughtful. 'I'm not sure. I used to talk. I can remember that quite clearly. I used to talk to *you*.' She scratched her ear with one hind foot. 'Where are we heading?'

'To the Palisades.'

'Well, that must be it, then.'

'What do you mean?'

'How should I know!' Nanny shook her head in annoyance. 'Get on with it,' she said.

I hadn't realised I'd stopped milking.

She went quiet after that and the only sound was the milk squirting into the mug. When I finished she nosed among the feed sacks and then began nibbling hay as if nothing had happened. The whole episode left me completely bewildered.

I lay back down and eventually I must have fallen asleep, because when I woke the wagon had stopped, the tailgate was down and Nanny was browsing at the side of the road. She lifted her head when I jumped down but she didn't speak. She looked perfectly normal. Perhaps I'd imagined she spoke to me. When you're road-weary and half asleep you can imagine all sorts of things. I wished I hadn't yelled out earlier. Luca probably thought I was mad.

We were a place called Nil. It wasn't much of a town. There was a ramshackle old mill with a small waterwheel and a handful of houses. The waterwheel was still and half the buildings had boards over the windows. The cook wagon was parked in the shade of an old peppercorn tree and Meridian was bending over a fire, stirring a pot. She looked up and waved. Stumpy's buggy was parked nearby and Luca was practising his rope tricks in front of it, watched by a ragged group of children. He jumped from left to right and each time the rope hit the ground, sparks flew. The children squealed with delight.

I went to put on my boots but I could only find one of them, the boot to my good foot. I was searching around the feedbags for its pair when Rye came by leading two horses.

'Bring your horse, Ellie. The trough's up here.'

I put the gunny sack over my shoulder and un-harnessed Sol.

'I hope he's not going to start talking too,' I muttered, glancing at Nanny.

'No chance of that. The horses never talked.'

I swung around. Nanny was nibbling a bit of dry bracken fern. She looked at me and blinked then she spat out the fern and put down her head, nosing about at the roots.

'Nanny, did you speak?'

There was no reply. I sidled past her and led Sol up the road, trying to keep calm. The stones were hot and they burnt my foot as I half hopped, half skipped after Rye. I hoped he'd be finished by the time I arrived. I didn't like people to see my bad foot.

Stumpy was standing at the trough, talking to Rye, his arms full of empty bottles.

'I think the boy's got a point,' he said. 'We need a pitchman, someone to ride ahead and drum up a crowd. We earned enough last night to buy an extra horse.'

'Luca's not old enough to travel alone.'

'Rubbish. When I was his age I was working the tent shows. I was my own man. It's no wonder he's chafing at the bit. You and Meridian hold him too close.'

'With good reason,' Rye replied.

Stumpy half filled a bottle with water then reached into his pocket and found a cork.

'When we reach Scarp I'll top these up with spirits. It's going to be a big night.'

I left Sol with Rye and headed over to the fire.

'Have you seen my boot, Meridian?'

'Isn't it in the feed wagon? Maybe it's near my seat.' She was watching Luca and she seemed a bit distracted. 'How did you sleep?' she asked.

'No good. I heard Nanny speak. I thought I was dreaming but I was wide awake.'

Meridian raised an eyebrow. 'Has it happened before?'

'I used to hear her all the time when I was small, but I thought I made it up.'

'It's not unusual, Ellie, not for us.'

'Us?'

'Way-people. The more I see you, the more I think you have a touch of the way in you.' She looked back at Luca and frowned. 'He's worse this morning. He's getting too big for his boots.'

'Then maybe he should take them off.'

I don't know why I said that. It just fell out.

Meridian shot me a startled look. 'He can't do that,' she said. 'He must never take off his boots.'

I don't know what she meant and I didn't ask. I headed to the way-wagon but my boot wasn't there.

Luca finished his practice and came over to me. 'Lost something?'

'My boot.'

'Maybe it walked?' He grinned and nodded towards the feed wagon. 'Have a look under the seat.'

There was a box under the wagon seat but it was locked.

'Open it!' I cried.

'What will you give me?'

Luca leaned against the running board.

'Where's that button-box? Is it in your sack? Give me a go of it,' he said.

I turned and walked away, wishing I'd been more careful. I should have kept the instrument hidden.

Meridian gave me bacon and beans for lunch and I sat eating with my foot tucked under me. I scowled at Luca. He had seemed so nice when I first met him but now he was the opposite.

'What are you looking at, Moonface?' he asked, as he wiped his plate with a slab of bread.

'Luca, what's come over you?' Meridian stood with her hands on her hips.

Luca shrugged. 'I've been talking to Stumpy,' he said. 'If I go ahead and spruik I'll have a big crowd waiting by the time the show arrives in Scarp. He agrees with me.'

'You're not going anywhere. You're not old enough or responsible enough to travel alone.'

'Well, *she's* travelling alone.' Luca tossed his head in my direction.

'Ellie's not alone. She's with us.'

'Luca, you're not pitching and that's final,' Rye said as he sat down on the step of the cook wagon.

Luca stomped off and I followed him. I wanted my boot.

'Give it back, Luca.'

'I will. But I want something in return.'

'You're not touching the button-box.'

He harnessed the horses and stepped up to the seat.

'It's going to be a long journey for you, being half shod,' he said. 'Do you want to change your mind?'

I took a deep breath. I wasn't going to let Luca push

me around, but I didn't see what I could do, short of physically forcing him to hand the boot over.

I climbed up onto the seat of the wagon and sat staring straight ahead, my arms folded over the gunny sack. 'I'll ride with you.'

'Suit yourself.'

Luca clicked his tongue and we moved off.

'Where do you think you're going, Luca?' Meridian called. 'Come here at once!'

'Horsefeathers!' Luca muttered as he stopped the wagon. 'It's not fair. They treat me like a child.'

I could have told him that he was acting like one, but I said nothing.

He went and talked to Meridian. I couldn't hear what was said but he came back sullen. He unlocked the box and threw my boot on the ground. I picked it up and went to join Meridian.

'Sorry about my nephew,' she said. 'We'll keep the button-box in the way-wagon. I'll lock it in the cupboard. You can have the key and you can get it whenever you want.'

'I won't want it, Meridian. Not until we reach the Trunk Road.'

✦

THE TOWN OF SCARP wasn't large but the medicine show drew an enormous crowd, even without Luca going ahead to pitch. He did his rope routine and Stumpy yelled through his mouth trumpet, promising that the Original Extract would cure anything. People queued six-deep around the stage and nearly everyone bought a bottle of the medicine. A big group waited outside Hannibal's tent, wanting to test their strength and pay for the privilege. May was kept busy doing tattoos and Rye sold all his lucky charms and set about carving more. He sat outside the way-wagon and chatted to people who were lining up to see Meridian. I sat with him.

'This medicine show came this way years ago. It was in my grandma's day,' a woman at the front of the queue said. 'Did this show ever have a rainmaker?'

'This show had all sorts of acts,' Rye answered. 'It was a big outfit in the old days.'

Just then Luca ran by, twirling his rope over his head. 'And it will be again!' he yelled as he passed.

The woman leaned close. 'But did it have a rain-maker?'

'One or two,' Rye answered vaguely. 'Charlatans, but they were entertaining enough.'

A man carrying a little boy came out of the wagon and Meridian stood at the door.

'Next,' she said. 'Ellie, would you like to help me?'

The lady asked Meridian the same question she'd asked Rye.

'Those fellas would lay claim to weather that was going to happen anyway,' Meridian said and she took the woman's hand.

'But I've heard of one,' the lady insisted. 'I think his name was Storm.'

'You're clutching at straws,' Meridian turned over the lady's hand and studied her palm. 'Rain will come,' she said. 'Your future is looking bright.'

AFTER A NIGHT in Scarp, we kept moving down the Sidling Road. Meridian said it would take us two weeks to reach the plains. Most of the places we passed through were too small to have names, but large crowds gathered wherever the medicine show stopped. Luca and Stumpy were thrilled, but the others were wary.

'It's not natural,' Rye said. 'What do you make of it, Meridian?'

Meridian said nothing. She'd told me the fewer who knew about the button-box the better. I was surprised she hadn't even told Rye.

Luca kept on at me, wanting to see it, but I wouldn't let him. I slept with my boots on and Meridian kept the door of the way-wagon locked whenever she wasn't there.

As we travelled, she began teaching me something of her craft. I would sit and watch her giving readings and making maps, and afterwards we'd discuss what she had said. She listened carefully to her customers and they always left satisfied. Sometimes I wondered if it was just the kindness that they paid for; other times I was amazed at what was revealed in the maps and the tea leaves.

Nanny spoke to me most mornings while I milked. I became used to hearing her voice but she annoyed me with her bossy ways.

'Remember that story you told me about the goat girl?' she said one day. 'You got it wrong.'

'How's that?'

'You probably weren't listening properly when I taught it to you.'

'You didn't teach it to me, Nanny. It was my story. I made it up.'

'Don't talk nonsense, Ellie. You couldn't make up a story like that. It was mine.'

'It was not!'

'Don't argue, my girl. You're starting the day on the wrong foot.' She turned her head and watched me milk. 'What's it like, doing the maps with the way-lady?' she asked.

'It's good,' I said. 'It reminds me of hunting fork root with Oma.'

Fork root was a bulb that grew in the deep gullies at home. It was good eating but was hard to find. The only sign above ground was a tiny flower that was almost too small to see but if you let your eyes go out of focus sometimes it would show itself.

'You were always good at that,' Nanny said. 'Better than Oma.' She let out a sigh. 'I doubt we'll ever see your grandmother again.'

'Don't say that!'

'I'm just being practical. You'd better prepare yourself, Ellie.'

The thought of never seeing Oma again took my breath away and made my heart hurt more than it should.

'She's not even your real grandmother,' I told myself. But that didn't stop me missing her.

Nanny gave me a nudge. 'You're talking to yourself,' she said. 'Keep your mind on the job.'

I changed teats and kept milking, listening to the sound of the squirting. I was also listening to an argument inside me. It was as if I was two girls in one. Half of me was hurt and angry; the other half was just plain lost.

'It's unforgivable,' the first girl said. 'Oma shouldn't have lied all those years.'

'Poor Oma,' the second half sighed, remembering how I slammed the door on the day I left.

'It's only what she deserved. She should have said you were adopted.'

The two girls pulled in different directions and by the time the mug filled up the only thing they could agree on was saving Oma's life.

I knew I wasn't travelling fast enough and that I'd be quicker alone, but I didn't want to leave the medicine show until I had to. Meridian offered me food and friendship and protection and I helped her in the way-wagon, making the tea, listening to people and trying my hand at the maps. May gave me a compass tattoo like Meridian's, a small one on the inside of my wrist. She used special ink that would only last a few months, and said if I wanted one that would last forever I'd need to come back to her when I was full grown.

I was just beginning to feel confident with the mapping when an unwelcome customer appeared: the man with no dust. I thought I'd seen the last of him. He stood at the door of the way-wagon late one evening, looking old and weary, more like when I'd first seen him on the road near the Trading Post. Maybe it was his weakened state that made Meridian let him in.

'Are you ill?' she asked.

'There you go again,' he wheezed, 'asking questions when you should be answering them.' He cleared his throat. 'I'm fine. Just a touch of dust cough. Nothing that a spot of music wouldn't fix.'

He glanced at Meridian's cupboard, then looked at me. For a moment it seemed that the cloud in his eye was swirling. It made me feel dizzy, yet it was hard to look away. I dropped my head and stared at the floor.

'What's your question?'

Meridian noticed him looking at me and her eyes narrowed. 'What are you after?'

'Rain,' he sighed. 'Same as everyone.'

I doubted that was true.

He focused again at the pictures on the wall, just like he had last time. I had the feeling he was drinking in everything he could learn. He pointed to one of the photos: a man standing on a suitcase painted with clouds. His hair was tied at the back and he wore a showman's smile. There was a lady behind him, holding a baby.

'There's a weatherman,' the fellow said. 'It's Pappy Storm.'

'Pappy's been dead many long years. That's not him,

that's his son. And he's not here.' Meridian took the picture and dropped it in my lap.

I stared at the photo. The lady wore a spangly skirt and a cowboy hat and boots. She was dancing and her dark hair swirled around her. She reminded me of Luca and so did the man.

I glanced up. The fellow seemed to have forgotten me. He was studying the wall of pictures. Suddenly he cleared his throat and stood up.

'Much obliged for the advice, ma'am,' he said.

'I haven't given any.'

'Nevertheless, a decision has been made.' He gave an odd little bow and left the wagon.

'Another satisfied customer!' I heard Stumpy yell.

17

The Weatherman

I PEERED THROUGH the window and watched the man-without-dust. He made his way through the crowd, heading to the place where the horses were tethered behind the wagons. He stopped near Sol. That worried me, so I left the way-wagon and skirted the crowd until I found a spot where I could keep an eye on my horse. The show was nearly over and Rye and Hannibal began taking down the tent.

I crouched behind the wheel of the cook wagon and peered through the spokes. I could see the fellow's boots with those strange lacings at the sides. He hummed a tune and tapped his pointy toe. Then he fell silent, but the toe kept tapping. A while later Luca came past, leading Rusty.

'Ah, here's the lad!' the man said to him. 'You're a fine hand with the lariat. Best act here.'

'Thanks, mister.' Luca was used to receiving compliments.

'Of course, that's not where your talent lies.'

'What?'

'Your grandaddy would turn in his grave if he knew you were wasting yourself on rope tricks.'

Luca stopped in his tracks.

'I never knew him.'

'Well that's a crying shame – there never was a better act than his. What a weatherman!'

'My pa was a rainmaker too. They say he had a good act.'

'Not as good as Pappy's.'

The man squatted and the back of his long coat lay in the dust. 'Pappy Storm could muster up rainclouds as if he was herding sheep. He was the real deal, a genuine rainmaker.'

'My pa was the same. He claimed to be the real thing. Some people might have believed it, but it was just a performance.'

'Maybe for your pa but not for your pappy. That fella could whistle up a storm at a moment's notice. That's how he got his name. Ask any old-timer round these parts.'

'Really?' Luca sat beside the man.

'I can't believe you don't know. You could probably do it too. It runs in the family.'

'Does it?'

'Course it does.' The man stood up. 'Nice meeting you, son.'

'Wait, mister—'

The fellow moved off and Rye called, 'Hurry up with that horse, Luca.'

I waited until Luca had hitched Rusty before I left my hiding place. I couldn't see the man. Rye was putting a collar on Sol and I went and gave my horse a pat.

'People are talking about Pappy,' Luca said to Rye.

'I know. The thirsty weather brings it on.'

'There no truth in it then?'

'Not a grain.'

'But they're not talking about Jimmy Thunder,' Luca said as he backed Sol into the shafts. He looked towards the buggy where Stumpy was selling the last few bottles of the elixir. 'This show could use a rainmaker. You reckon my pa will ever come back?'

'Not likely.' Rye stepped up onto the seat. 'Ellie, what say you travel with me this evening?'

Rye's wagon had CHARMS FOR ALL OCCASIONS written on the side in fancy letters that looked like they were carved out of wood. I climbed up beside him.

'Another good night,' he said. 'I should be happy, but I'm not.'

He slapped the reins and we pulled out onto the road.

'It just doesn't add up. All these people appearing out of nowhere and spending what little they have.' Rye stuffed his pipe and lit it, looking at the road ahead.

'Where's Luca's pa, Rye?' I asked.

'My brother cleared out a while ago. I don't know where he is. His stage name was Jimmy Thunder. Why?'

'Just wondering. What about Luca's ma?'

'Hannah Savanah. She was a dancer. She died, Ellie. Killed in an accident when Luca was just shy of three years old. We don't talk about it much.'

'Why not?'

'It doesn't pay to bring up sad memories. Do you drive?'

'Of course.'

Rye handed me the reins and reached into a bag that hung on a peg behind him. He took out a knife and a small piece of wood and began whittling.

'Do your charms work, Rye?'

'They're just trinkets. People buy them for gifts. I don't think they've ever brought good luck, but then again they haven't brought bad luck, either.' He laughed. 'Nobody's ever followed the troupe to complain about my charms the way they complain about Stumpy's medicine.'

The road ahead grew steep and I could see lights way below.

'Is that Brink?' I asked.

'Horseshoe Bend. After that it's Brink, and then we're almost on the plains.'

He concentrated on the wood and I asked him how he could see in the dark.

'Do it by feel,' he replied. 'Same as Meridian with the mapping.'

'Have you always done carving?'

'Always.'

'How come you didn't become a weatherworker like your pa?'

'Didn't want to. I like the charms.'

'Could your father really make it rain?'

Rye looked up. 'You ask a lot of questions. I guess that's how it is with the way. You've got to ask the questions before you can work out the answers. Meridian says you're doing really well.'

'I like it, Rye. I wish I could stay.'

'Nothing stopping you, is there?'

'I have to take the Trunk Road west. It's because my grandma is ill.'

'Then shouldn't you be home with her?'

'I can't.'

'Why not?'

There was no easy answer to that. My home wasn't my home anymore. I couldn't be with Oma because she'd done me wrong and I'd stormed off. But I'd done her wrong as well, a terrible wrong. I hated to think of her lying in the back room of the shack, so sick and old.

Rye waited for me to speak but everything was knotted up in me like a skein of tangled wool.

'It's complicated, Rye.'

'Families often are.'

Something about Rye's soft voice brought a lump to my throat. 'I should be home with my oma, but she's not really my grandmother. All my life I thought she was, and then I found out she's not even related. But I can't stop loving her just like that, and I have to try and fix her. And just maybe along the way I can find my real family.'

Rye drew on his pipe. It glowed cherry red in the dark.

'I think she's dying,' I added quietly.

He looked away. 'I'm sorry, Ellie.'

We were silent for a while. Then he asked me if I'd like a charm. 'Not that I can guarantee it'll work.'

I nodded, fighting back my tears.

He was searching in his bag for the right piece of wood when we came to a sharp bend. Rye took back the reins. 'This is the first turn of the switchback. Seven more to go, then it levels out at Horseshoe Bend.'

'Luca's ma – what sort of accident was it?' The question surprised me. It seemed to come out of my mouth before I'd even thought it. It surprised Rye too, and perhaps that's why he answered it so readily.

'She got struck by lightning. Killed instantly. It could have been Luca.'

Rye turned to me. 'I'd be obliged if you'd forget I said that, Ellie. It's not something to be shared.'

'Why not?'

'Luca doesn't know.' He cleared his throat and handed me the reins again. Then he worked away at the wood.

'How come?'

The knife slipped when I said that and Rye drew in his breath. He put his finger in his mouth.

'Are you hurt?'

'It's just a nick.'

'Maybe I asked the wrong question?'

'Or the right one.'

Rye didn't say anything for a long time. I watched the moon rise in the east and waited for him to continue. Perhaps it was my silence that drew the story from him.

'Jimmy was fooling around at the time, playing with Luca. He handed him a sky rod and that's how it happened. He could have handed the kid anything from his kit – a rain drum, the wind howler, a thunder clapper – it was just bad luck that he handed him the sky rod. Then he held Luca up in the air. Luca's ma saw what was going to happen. She leapt up and took the rod and that's when she got hit.'

'What's a sky rod, Rye?'

'A lightning stick. Harmless in most people's hands, but deadly if...'

'—you've got the gift. So Jimmy was a real weatherman?'

'Heck, no! Jimmy couldn't stir up a storm to save himself. He wanted to though. He couldn't wait to turn fourteen because that's when the gift comes through, but his birthday arrived and nothing happened. He set himself up as a rainman anyway. He got the gear and worked up a showy act. It was entertaining enough, but he didn't have what it takes.'

'What does it take?'

'The gift and the knowledge about how to use it. Pappy did it with his hands.'

I would have liked to ask Rye how, but he was on a roll as sure as the wagon wheels were rolling down the road, and I didn't want to interrupt.

'Jimmy didn't know what he was doing. It was a terrible mistake.'

'You mean *Luca* pulled the lightning?' I asked quietly.

Rye nodded. 'Meridian reckons the gift skipped a generation. Ever since Luca was born he showed the signs – watching the clouds, studying the ants. When he cut his first teeth he was whistling through them, calling up the winds. But there was nobody to teach him and a gift like that is dangerous, so we headed him off at the pass as quick as we could by getting him into the rope work.'

Rye paused.

'You're like Meridian,' he said. 'All she has to do is wait and I tell her everything.'

'Is that why Luca wears those rubber boots, to protect him from the lightning?'

I don't think Rye heard me. He was leaning sideways off the seat and looking up at the road above.

'Who's that travelling with the boy?' he asked. 'I've told him before not to give anyone a ride at night.'

There wasn't much light from the moon, but even in the dark, I guessed who it was.

Rye turned back and stared at the road ahead. 'The boots? Yes, they're to protect him. The rubber is meant to stop the lightning. But the greatest protection is not knowing what Pappy Storm could do.'

'Well, he knows now,' I said.

'What?' Rye stopped the wagon. We were halfway

to the third bend of the switchback and the road was narrow, with a solid rock wall on one side and a sheer drop on the other. There was no place to pull over.

I heard the other wagons stopping behind us.

'How could he know?' Rye stared at me in shock.

'What's happening?' Meridian called. She walked down the road towards us. 'Why have you stopped, Rye? This isn't a good spot.'

Rye put his head in his hands. 'Luca knows,' he whispered to himself. 'There'll be no holding him now.'

18

The Horse Thief

WE ARRIVED IN Horseshoe Bend just before dawn and Rye asked me to unharness his horse and to look after Rusty as well. He and Meridian wanted to speak to Luca in the way-wagon. They were gone for a long time and when Luca came out he had a wild look in his eye and his jaw was set. He stomped off in the direction of Stumpy's buggy.

I was leading Sol to water when Meridian came and spoke to me.

'Luca won't tell us anything,' she said. 'He won't say a word. I don't know who that fellow is or what he's up to, but if anything happens to my nephew...'

Her bottom lip trembled and I thought she was going to cry. I took her hand.

A short time later Luca came running along the line of wagons.

'Meeting,' he called. 'Stumpy's buggy in five minutes.'

'Since when does Luca call the meetings?' Hannibal asked as he walked past.

Everyone gathered around the buggy.

'There's been a change of plan,' Stumpy said. 'We're going west once we hit Brink. The lad here tells me that's where the really big crowds will be. There's a fair on out that way.'

'No, Stumpy. We'll go to Holman's Flat as planned,' Meridian said. 'There's nothing but heat and misery in the west.'

'Exactly. That's why we'll make a killing.'

'What are you talking about?' Rye stood with his arms folded.

'Got to change with the times. Give the customers what they want.' Stumpy grinned at Luca. 'The boy's working up a new act.'

'He'll never top the roping,' Hannibal said. 'What sort of act?'

'Rainmaking.'

Hannibal gave a hoot. 'I don't think that's a good idea. Folks won't take kindly to the boy making light of their misfortune. Anyway, the show's going great guns as it is.'

'It could be greater,' Luca said. 'And I won't promise what I can't deliver.'

He stared accusingly at Rye. 'Why did you keep it from me?'

'Luca, you don't know what you're playing with here.'

'I do know!'

'You're not changing your act. I won't allow it.'

Meridian put her hand on Luca's arm but he shook her off.

'You won't let me do anything,' he cried. 'You won't let me pitch. You won't even let me choose my own boots.'

'There's truth in what the boy says,' Stumpy told Meridian. 'You can't keep him tied to your apron strings. He's got to be allowed to make his own way. When I was his age—'

'Stay out of it, Stumpy. This is family business.' Rye stood beside Meridian.

'Whatever happens in the troupe is my business. Give the lad his head. If he wants to change his act, it's his decision.'

'Luca's not changing his act,' Meridian said firmly. 'And this medicine show is not heading west.'

'Then I'll go by myself!' Luca announced.

'You're not going anywhere.' Meridian took her nephew's arm and this time she held him tight. Rye went to the other side of him and the two of them marched Luca away, heading up the road.

'Meeting adjourned,' Stumpy said, trying to get some control of the situation. 'We'll continue later.'

He went inside his buggy and closed the door.

It was time for me to milk and I was heading towards Nanny when I heard Luca shouting.

'You're just a bunch of fools! You can't see an opportunity when it's staring you in the face.'

'Fools or not, the answer's no! It's for your own good,' Rye shouted back.

Luca pulled away and ran back to the wagons. Meridian and Rye didn't follow. Rye took Meridian's arm and they kept walking.

Luca rushed towards me. 'Ellie, I need to ask you something, a favour.'

'What is it?'

'Can you sell me your horse? I've got plenty of money.' He jingled the coins in his pocket.

'Sol's not for sale.'

'Hire him then. I'll bring him back, I promise.'

'No, Luca. I can't do that. Sol belongs to my brother. And besides, I need him myself.'

He kicked the ground. 'I need to get away,' he said. 'They're holding me back and I can't stand it any longer.'

'I've got to milk my goat,' I said, but as soon as Luca left I went after Meridian and Rye. They had their heads together and I think Meridian was crying.

I was halfway up the road when I heard Sol neigh. I looked back and saw his tail behind the feed wagon, swishing from side to side. He was backing up. I ran to him and when I reached the wagon I saw him rear. A saddle slipped off his back and landed on the ground with a thump. It wasn't my saddle.

'What's going on?' I cried.

Sol was pawing the ground, his ears laid flat on his neck, and Luca was standing before him, edging away. I reckon if I hadn't arrived when I did, Sol would have trampled him.

'What are you doing?'

With a sidelong glance at my horse, Luca grabbed the saddle and was gone.

It took me a while to settle Sol. I was inside the feed wagon filling him a hay net when I heard Stumpy shout, 'Get off that mare at once!'

A moment later, Luca galloped off on Stumpy's pony. I looked up the road and saw him race past Meridian and Rye, raising a cloud of dust. Meridian let out a cry of dismay and Rye started running, but anyone could see it was useless. He stopped after a few paces and when Meridian caught up with him he put his arm around her. She rested her head on his shoulder and they watched until Luca was out of sight. Then they turned and walked slowly back to the wagons.

I fed Sol and was about to start the milking when I heard a shout. It was Meridian. I ran to the way-wagon. The door hung off its hinges. And so did the cupboard door. The button-box was gone.

Meridian's face was red and she ran her fingers through her hair.

'Don't panic, love,' Rye said. 'We'll catch up with him. Just keep calm.'

'Calm before the storm,' Meridian said. 'Oh, Rye.'

'There'll be no storms. There'll be nothing like that.'

'That's wishful thinking and you know it.' Tears rolled down her cheeks. She looked up at me standing in the doorway.

'I have to go,' I said. 'I have to go right now.'

I turned and ran back to my horse. Nanny was beside him.

'Where are we going?' she asked as I threw on Sol's saddle.

'After them!'

Rye came running over, carrying a waterbag.

'Take this.' He strapped it to Sol's chest.

Meridian joined us, puffy faced and panting. She'd run from the cook wagon, where she'd filled a sack with supplies. She stuffed it into my saddlebag as Rye helped me mount.

'There's a turn-off beyond the township that will take you directly to the Trunk Road.' She reached up and put her hand on my arm. 'Look after yourself, Ellie. And if possible, can you look after Luca as well?'

'What do you mean?'

'Don't let him take off his boots. His life may depend on it, the way your oma's life depends on that instrument.'

'I'll try,' I promised. But I wasn't thinking about Luca. I just needed to get the button-box back.

I leaned down and hugged Meridian goodbye. I hugged Rye as well, and when I let him go he reached into his pocket and pulled out a charm: a tiny, delicate wishbone. I slipped it into my pocket then turned and galloped away, my heart pounding to the rhythm of Sol's hoofbeats.

PART THREE

19

The Plains

THE TURN-OFF WAS only minutes beyond Horse-shoe Bend, a dusty track that wound through the foothills. I passed an old orchard and a couple of poor-looking farms and when I came over a rise I saw Luca ahead. He wasn't alone anymore; the fellow was riding behind him. He must have been waiting for Luca just out of town.

I knew I could easily catch up to them. Sol was strong and twice the size of Stumpy's mare, and although the pony was moving fast, she wouldn't keep up that pace for long with two people on her back. I planned to stay out of sight and wait until they had stopped for the night before I approached. I couldn't see how I could help Luca, not when he was with that man. I would get the button-box and go.

I slowed Sol to a trot and Nanny came panting along-side me. Her sides heaved and her tongue hung out.

'I'm not the goat I used to be,' she gasped.

I paused to let her catch her breath and looked back. The switchback zigzagged above us. There were peaks in the distance and, very far away, I could just make out the pass. Spit Farm seemed a world away.

'I wouldn't bank on Luca giving up that button-box without a fight,' Nanny panted. 'Not after what that fellow told him.'

'What did he tell him?'

'To steal it along with the horse. Told him he'd be needing it for the journey and that he wouldn't get far without it.'

'How do you know?'

'I had my head against the front boards of the feed wagon. I heard everything that man said. He filled the boy's head with dreams. Told him he'd be a star at Stolt and couldn't fail. Told him he had a special gift and that his family had lied to him for years because they wanted to keep him close.'

'It's true,' I said, looking at the track ahead.

The pony disappeared into some trees and I urged Sol on. The sun was up and already the day was hot.

'You go ahead,' Nanny panted. 'I'll catch you up.'

The track entered a pine forest and the shade was a welcome relief. I slowed Sol to a trot, then a walk, as I didn't want to get too close. When I heard voices I slipped to the ground and told Sol to stay where he was. The pony's hoofprints left the track and veered into the pines. I heard the faint sound of water and moved cautiously forward, hiding behind the trees.

The mare was standing up to her fetlocks in a creek, drinking, and Luca squatted beside her. She was in a lather of sweat and looked done in. Luca's face was flushed. He splashed water on himself and drank deeply.

'Don't you want a drink, mister?' he asked.

'Later.'

The man sat leaning against a tree trunk. He looked as exhausted as the pony.

'You could have saddled her,' he said in his wheezy voice. 'It doesn't suit me riding bareback.'

'There wasn't time.'

'Nevermind, we'll get a saddle on the way. At least you got the most important thing.'

My gunny sack lay at his feet. He looked at it and gave a rattling sigh. 'Give us a tune, boy. Let's see what we can do for ourselves.'

'It's broken and I can't play.'

'Makes no difference.'

Luca scrambled up the bank and when he picked up the button-box my heart missed a beat. *Don't!* I wanted to yell, but I bit my lip. I heard the click as he released the catch. The sound filled me with dread – but there was nothing I could do. He sat down to play.

The man closed his eyes and breathed deeply. The weariness fell from him. He took off his big hat and ran his fingers through his hair, which was grey but surprisingly thick and shiny. Then he stood and stretched as if waking from a long sleep. 'Ah, that's better,' he said. 'Now, play for the mare.'

Luca turned towards the pony. She had stopped

drinking and stood with her head low, staring listlessly into the creek. When he played in her direction she lifted her nose, sniffed the air and whinnied. She pawed the water, shook herself and then, in two strides, she was up the bank, looking fresh and ready to go.

'And yourself, a few notes for yourself.'

Luca played, and when the fellow raised his hands the button-box stopped.

'Come on. Your future's waiting for you,' he said.

Luca jumped onto the mare's back and the man-without-dust leapt on behind, agile as a boy.

They turned back to the track and as they cantered away the man looked over his shoulder and smiled. I quickly ducked my head behind the tree trunk.

ᏋᏋ

THE COUNTRY BEYOND the forest had no shade other than a few stands of ash trees. The track was undulating and I could see no sign of the mare. I didn't want to ride Sol hard during the heat of the day so we settled for a loping sort of trot, and Nanny caught up with us. By mid-afternoon I'd emptied my waterbag, and needed to find water for my animals. I was relieved when we came to a settlement, a tiny town of half a dozen buildings. Most of them were empty, but the place had a storehouse and I went inside and asked if there was a trough. A pouchy-looking man sat behind the counter fanning himself with a newspaper.

'The well's around the back,' he said. 'If this weather keeps up I'm going to have to charge for water. Where are you heading?'

'West,' I said. 'To the cattle fair.'

'You're the third today. I'll tell you what I told the others. It's not worth going to that fair. If it's hot here it'll be worse out west.'

'Did you see a boy with long black hair?'

'What a showman! He was boasting about his rainmaking act. I don't know what his mate did, some sort of performer dressed up in old-time costume.'

The man led me behind the building. The bucket clanked on the sides of the well and it went a long way before it hit the water. It came up half full.

'When was that boy here?' I asked.

'A couple of hours back. Are you tracking him?'

I nodded.

'Well, he won't go far in this heat. There's a spring further on. I expect you'll catch him there. You'll see the trees from the track.'

❧

I RODE ON, but I didn't see any trees or spring. The track forked and I must have taken the wrong turn, because the sun sank low in the sky and there was no sign of Luca.

I was hot and tired and the thought of the button-box getting further away made me feel sick in my stomach. What a fool I'd been to let it out of my sight.

'Don't be too hard on yourself, girl,' Nanny said. 'You've had a lot to contend with. You'll feel better after you've eaten. What's in the bag?'

We stopped beside an old hay shed. There was nothing around except empty paddocks. The fence posts threw long shadows in the late afternoon sun.

Meridian had given me six oatcakes and a stack of flapjacks left over from dinner the night before. I took out two of the cakes and offered one to Nanny.

'They're for you,' she said.

'But Nanny, you've hardly eaten anything.'

'Do as you're told.'

I ate one oatcake and put the other away. I looked along the track.

'We should go back to the settlement. We need directions.'

'No, Ellie. We're staying here. You're tired and you need to rest.'

'We can't stop. He'll get away.'

'I'd prefer you didn't argue,' she said calmly. 'Unsaddle the horse. We'll sleep in the shed.'

'No, we won't.'

Nanny clicked her tongue and gave a little sigh. 'It's my responsibility to look after you, Ellie. It'll be dark soon and I'm not having you travelling at night.'

'You're not the one in charge, Nanny.'

'No,' she said, 'but you have a long way to go and you've got to pace yourself.'

There was sense in that. I unsaddled Sol and took out my shawl, then lay down next to my saddlebags.

I was tired, but I couldn't sleep. Every time I shut my eyes I saw Stumpy's pony galloping into the night.

When Nanny sat down beside me I rested my head on her shoulder.

'Would a story help?' she asked. 'You loved my tales when you were little.'

'They were mine, not yours,' I said wearily.

Nanny ignored me. 'Remember the story of Gola and Gabe?'

I nodded.

'They were promised,' she said. 'They'd been friends since childhood, but one day, when the promise time drew near, somebody else arrived.'

That wasn't in my story but I didn't say anything. It was getting dark and I pulled my shawl around me and snuggled close.

'Gola was out with the goats when she saw him in the distance. She knew everyone in the Gleam country and this man was a stranger. The kids lifted their heads and sniffed the air, the way they did when they caught the scent of a range-cat, but Gola was curious. She merged with the goats so he couldn't see her. It was a power she had. She took on the appearance of the animals around her as she made her way towards him.

'He was a young man, but not as young as Gabe, and he was sitting on a rock making something from a piece of hollow stick. She crept closer and watched him work. His hands were fine and skilful and he worked with the simplest of tools, sanding the wood smooth and then punching a row of holes. When he lifted the stick to his lips Gola smiled with delight, for he'd made a tiny flute. It wasn't long before she revealed herself and spoke to him. She learned his name was Harland and that he'd come from the outside world. After that day she visited him often. She didn't tell anybody she'd met him, not her mother and not Gabe.'

I was getting sleepy. I forgot about the button-box for a while and listened to the story.

'There was a cave where Gola and her mother shut the goats at night so they could milk them in the morning. One night the goat girl invited her new friend to meet her there. As luck would have it, Gabe chose to visit on that same evening.'

Nanny paused and looked at the sky. She blinked and nodded to herself. 'Yes, I think this is how it goes,' she said. 'It's one of the old tales, the legends, from back in the shining time. Everyone knew it.'

'Who's everyone?'

Nanny didn't answer. She cocked her head, first to one side and then the other as if she was listening.

'He was full of fun, that Gabe,' she continued. 'He planned to surprise the goat girl and he smuggled himself into the cave. He didn't merge – he didn't know how. Instead, he wore a goats' wool coat and slipped between two animals, keeping his head low. He waited until she'd secured the gate and then he leapt out, laughing.

'It was the sort of prank Gola usually enjoyed, but she didn't enjoy it that night. She said some cursing words that made the coat stick fast to him. He laughed even louder, and this annoyed her so she said more words, stronger words, and soon the coat was not just sticking to Gabe, it was part of him. It was his own skin and he was standing on four legs, not two.'

I smiled to myself. 'This is a good story, Nanny. It's better than mine.'

'Good or bad, who can say? I can't recall the end right now. Maybe I never knew it.' She cocked her head again. It was some time before she went on.

'The boy could no longer speak. When he tried to talk, all that came out was a forlorn bleat. And the only difference between him and the other goats was a strand of red wool between his horns, the string that he used to wear around his neck.

'The goat girl realised she'd gone too far. She tried to turn him back but she didn't know how, so she went to fetch her mother. Her mother was wise. All her life she'd drunk the milk of their fabulous herd. There was nothing she didn't know and no problem she couldn't solve.'

I ran my fingers through Nanny's hair. It was soft and curly and although it was nothing like Oma's hair, it made me remember being with my grandmother. I wished I hadn't left the way I did. I hadn't even said goodbye. But it was too late now. I closed my eyes and went to sleep to the murmur of Nanny's voice.

20

The Trunk Road

WE SET OFF at sunrise the next morning. Nanny insisted that all we need do was find the Trunk Road and Luca would be on it.

I knew the road went from east to west so I figured if we tracked due south we would hit it. The trail we were on passed through country that must once have grown wheat. Deep ditches ran on either side of the track and irrigation channels led from them into the fields. Shirley Serpentine had told me about the wheat fields of the plains. She said the soil was rich and deep and by rights belonged to us because it had all been washed down from the mountains. It didn't look rich and deep here. The further we went, the drier the land became. A thin layer of dust blew across the hardpan and occasionally I saw the bones of some animal that had got stuck in the mud as the water in the channels dried up.

The day was hot and by mid-morning I had drained

the waterbag. Sweat ran into my eyes and I felt my lips burning. I pulled Pop's hat down low and hunched forward in the saddle.

'How much further, Nanny?'

She sniffed the air and her nostrils quivered. 'To the Trunk Road? I don't know. But there's water nearby.'

She veered off the trail towards an old sagewood tree. Beneath it, she found a soak, a marshy patch with some groundwater – not a lot, but enough to quench our thirst.

'I went to sleep before you reached the end of that story,' I told Nanny as I refilled the waterbag.

'Me too,' she said. 'Maybe we'll hear some more tonight.'

'*Hear* some more? What do you mean?'

'It's coming to me, Ellie, and I'm not sure if I'm remembering or if I'm hearing it for the first time.'

I strapped the waterbag back on Sol's chest and we continued at a steady pace. When the road passed a ridge, Nanny suggested we get a better view. She headed up a rocky slope and Sol followed, picking his way among the stones. From the top we had a wide view of the flatlands. They seemed to stretch forever. I could see a tiny settlement to the south. Beyond it, a wide, straight road ran across the country like a scar – the Trunk Road.

We went down the far side of the ridge and met the track again. It wasn't long before I noticed fresh cow pats. I couldn't see the cattle until we were almost upon them, such was the dust they were raising, and then

I was surprised there were so few – just a dozen thin cows and a couple of steers. They walked slowly with their heads low, taking no notice of the dog that was nipping their heels. A woman on a solid little cow pony was with them. I cantered to catch up with her. She had a long plait down her back. Her hair was copper coloured and it caught the sun.

'Are you going to the Trunk Road?' I asked.

She looked me up and down. 'All hat, no herd,' she remarked. 'Course I'm going to the Trunk Road.'

She glanced at my waterbag. I noticed her own bag hung limp and empty around the pony's neck, so I untied mine and handed it over. She seemed a bit surprised. She drank deeply, gulping it down.

'I was hoping there'd be water at Bygone Junction but the well there had dried up.' She wiped her mouth with the back of her hand and drank again. 'Just you, is it?' she asked.

I nodded, although it felt like there were three of us – Sol, Nanny and me.

'Have you been on the Trunk before?' she said.

I shook my head.

'It's the best drove road in the country. It used to have waterholes all the way along but they're drying up.'

'Are you a herder?'

She wiped her brow and looked over the heads of the cattle. 'I am now but I probably won't be for much longer.'

I stared hard at her. It was difficult to tell how old she was. Her skin was like dried leather but her body looked young and strong.

'You've got a searching look to you, child. Tell me what you're about.'

'I was with some herders,' I said. 'Twelve years ago.'

She pushed back her hat and squinted at me. 'Herders don't usually travel with young, not babies anyway. What were their names?'

'I don't know.'

She handed me the waterbag and nodded her thanks.

'I think I might be a herder,' I told her. 'I have to find out about them.'

'You could ask Rush when you get to the fair. He's the boss man. He knows everyone on the stock routes.'

She whistled to her dog and the pony moved off.

'Wait,' I cried. 'Do you mean the cattle fair?'

'That's the one,' she said. 'They're holding it at Stolt.'

'That's where I'm going.'

She looked at me over her shoulder then she brought the pony to a halt. 'You can travel with me if you like.'

There was nothing I would have liked more, but the cows were moving slowly and I had to travel fast.

I thanked her for the offer and cantered ahead. Nanny ran beside me.

'I'd rather you didn't speak to strangers,' she said. 'There could be all sorts on the roads these days.'

'Nanny, do you remember the herders that left me at Spit Farm?'

'Vaguely.'

'What were their names?'

'Names? How would I know?'

'Would you recognise them if you saw them?'

'They were people like any other. There was a boy whose job it was to make sure I kept up with the mob. I think he may have milked me. But don't ask me to pick one herder from the next. It would be like picking a single sheep in a flock, or one cow out of a herd.'

We began to meet other travellers. Most were heading in the same direction and by mid-afternoon we reached the settlement I'd seen from the ridge. A sign on the roadside said 'Last stop before Slattern Creek'. There was a blacksmith's shop and a row of stores on the main street. I asked the blacksmith if he'd seen Luca and he sent me next door to a place that sold rope and saddlery.

'This morning,' the woman behind the counter said. 'Best day we've had in weeks. Sold him a saddle and a pair of boots. They'd sat on the shelf for years gathering dust – they were too fancy for folks round here. He reckoned they had his name on them.'

'What was his name?' I asked.

'Luca the Lightning Lad. Reckoned he was going to break the drought once he got to Stolt.' The lady laughed and shook her head.

There was a post office next to the saddlery. I went inside and used Oma's coin to buy paper, an envelope and a stamp. Meridian had said my grandmother would be out of her mind with worry. I wanted to put her mind at rest.

Dear Oma, I wrote. *I'm heading to the Trunk Road and I'm safe and well. I hope to put everything right as soon as I can. Nanny is with me. I drink fresh milk every day and every night I sleep under the shawl and think of you.*

My eyes stung when I wrote that and so I crossed it out and started again on a fresh piece of paper.

Dear Oma. Don't worry about me. I'm fine. I'm going to fix the button-box. Thank you for the shawl. It's come in handy because the nights are cool.

I didn't want to say I'd lost the button-box so I didn't write much more.

Nanny is well and so is Sol. Tell Tod it's only a lend. I'll bring his horse home soon.

Love Ellie

xxx

I addressed the envelope care of the Trading Post, via Sidling Road, Mt Ossa, knowing that nobody in my family would be likely to pick up mail from there any time soon. Still, it made me feel better to have written it.

ONCE WE MET the Trunk Road we came across many more travellers. Some had cattle and some didn't. Some were on horseback, others on foot. There were drays, wagons and handcarts. Nanny and I received many curious looks.

'We'll stop and rest at the first suitable spot,' Nanny said. 'Then we'll travel at night, when it's safer.'

'I thought you didn't want me travelling at night.'

She turned off the road and followed a path into some scrub. We settled down to rest in a hollow that might have once been a dam.

My dinner was oatcakes soaked in milk. Once I'd finished them I tried not to start on the flapjacks, but half of them were gone before I could stop myself.

The day had been fearfully hot, but as soon as the sun went down I was shivering. There was plenty of wood about for a fire but I had nothing to start it with. I was lucky to have my shawl. I gathered brush for a mattress and made myself comfortable.

'How did the story end, Nanny?' I asked, when she came and sat beside me.

'Let's see… They came running, I know that much. Gola and her mother ran to the goat cave but when they arrived they couldn't find him.'

I scratched Nanny behind the ear and she yawned with pleasure.

'There was no sign of the goat with the red wool around its horns,' she said. 'He seemed to have disappeared. Gola thought he might have jumped the gate and she went looking for him, wandering over the hills and calling his name, but he was nowhere to be found.'

Nanny stood up and walked around the edge of the hollow.

'What happened to him?' I asked.

She began muttering to herself and shaking her head as if she wanted to shake something out of it. Then she stopped and scratched her flank.

'Perhaps I've got this story wrong. What did I say his name was?'

'Gabe.'

'Not him, the other fellow.'

'Harland.'

'Yes, that's the one. That man had been there in the cave before the goats arrived and he'd seen everything that happened. When Gola went to get her mother, Harland slipped from his hiding place and grabbed the goat with the red thread.'

'Why?'

Nanny lowered her voice. 'It's hardly a bedtime tale, Ellie. I don't like the way it's heading.'

She came down the bank and stood close to me. She was trembling and her breath made little puffs in the night air.

'Are you cold, Nanny? Have some shawl.'

'Harland killed that goat and took it away to his camp.' Nanny spoke quietly, almost under her breath. 'There were signs – broken bushes and a trail of blood – but nobody noticed. Gola kept searching. She had no idea that she would never see her friend again.'

Nanny gave a shuddering sigh. 'The moon's up,' she said. 'Saddle your horse and we'll be on our way.'

I hadn't slept. I'd hardly had a rest, but my goat was ready to move on.

'When I used to tell that story they lived happily ever after. They had three perfect children and—'

'That's not what happened,' Nanny said.

I reached up and held her face in my hands. 'Why are you telling this story?'

'I don't know,' she whispered. 'Pack up, my girl. We haven't got all night. They can't be far ahead. If we make good time this evening you'll catch them by morning.'

I put the story out of my mind. It had nothing to do with me.

21

Slattern Creek

I'D NEVER SEEN a road as broad as the Trunk Road. Three carts could travel abreast and at night, when it was empty, it seemed even wider. Occasionally I saw campfires flickering in the dark and heard cattle moving in the scrub. Now and then a dog barked. Apart from that, the only sound was Sol's hoofbeats. The moon was nearly half full and it was stained red from the dust in the air.

I rode with my shawl wrapped tight around me, one hand on my saddle horn and the other holding the reins. From time to time the smooth movement of Sol's gait lulled me to sleep and I slumped forward, only to wake with a start.

'Keep your wits about you, girl,' Nanny said.

She was wide awake. She seemed to have more energy now than when we'd left Horseshoe Bend. She trotted with her head held high and her eyes fixed on the west, not that there was anything to see except for the road, the horizon and the huge sky above.

'Look up,' she said. 'Keep your eyes on the stars. It'll stop you falling asleep.'

I did as she said. The stars were coming out in clusters, the same stars I knew from home, only here they looked lonely and further away.

My neck began to ache so I stared between Sol's ears instead. The road seemed to glow slightly as if it had taken in the light of the day and was slowly releasing it.

'Will we travel all night?' I asked.

'We'll see.'

I was too tired to sit up straight in the saddle, so I leaned along Sol's mane and clasped his neck. From the corner of my eye I could see Nanny's white shape beside me. She went faster as the night wore on.

I was getting sleepy, falling into that state when your mind becomes vast as the night sky and all sorts of things pass through it. I thought I heard Nanny talking.

'Poor child. Her grandmother would never allow it. I shouldn't allow it.'

'What's that, Nanny?' I murmured.

'A young girl sleeping on the move and hearing tales no child should ever hear.'

I realised she wasn't talking to me, she was talking to herself.

'Harland!' she cried. 'Curse that name.'

She put on a burst of speed as if to leave the name behind. But maybe it was ahead of her, because as she travelled through the night it grew louder in her mind, and so did the story. I heard it all, how the goat girl had no more thoughts for Harland because she was worried about her friend Gabe, how her promise day came and went without any trace of the goat with the red thread, and how, for weeks, she stayed clear of Harland – but he didn't stay clear of her.

Nanny's mind was full of the tale and I heard it as clearly as if she was speaking in my ear. *Harland put flowers near the entrance to the cave and left gifts at the door of her hut – herbs and wild berries, eggs he'd robbed from nests, fish he'd caught from the stream near his camp. He was intent on winning her favour and the more she refused him, the more intent he became.*

I was vaguely aware that Nanny was drawing ahead of me.

'Slow down,' I thought, as her voice grew faint.

He decided to make her a present she couldn't refuse. He was skilled with his hands and had everything he needed, all the materials to make the perfect gift.

Nanny gave a startled cry and I came to my senses. Had I been dreaming? She stood nearby, staring away from the road. Sol stopped beside her.

'Can you hear that?' she asked.

I sat up and stretched. I couldn't hear anything except a calf bawling off to the north, and somewhere the creaking of a windmill.

'It's just a calf,' I said.

'No. Further on – the crying. I'd know that sound anywhere. Oh, the poor dears!'

The sky was light and I wondered how long we'd been travelling. It would be dawn soon.

Nanny began running along the road and Sol had to canter to keep up.

'Wait, Nanny. Stop!' I yelled.

She took no notice. There was a settlement ahead. I could see wagons by the roadside and the roofs of a few buildings.

'I'll be back. Wait for me at the town.'

She let out a loud bleat and left the Trunk Road, disappearing into the scrubby country on the verge. I saw her white tail bob up and down among the bushes and before long she was out of sight.

✺

NOBODY WAS AWAKE at Slattern Creek. Travellers, camped on the roadside, were lying around their fires, and other people were asleep on the verandahs of the buildings. It wasn't a big town, but it was big enough to have a way-house and stables, and I was looking for a trough when a lady appeared with a lantern.

'You're either very early or too late,' she said. 'What do you want?'

'Just water for my horse.'

She showed me the trough.

'Now that I'm up I might as well fix breakfast,' she said. 'Will you be eating?' She held the lantern to my face.

I still had one of Oma's coins so I said I would. The

lady told me she'd call me when it was ready.

I was worried about Sol. He'd hardly eaten anything since we left Horseshoe Bend. I decided I'd better skip breakfast and use the money for horse feed. I went after the lady and found her in the way-house kitchen, frying bacon in a skillet.

'I can't afford breakfast. Do you have oats? I need to feed my horse.'

'Have both,' she said. 'It's already paid for.'

'What?'

'Fella with a boy left the money, said to feed you up good and proper. Will you be wanting a bed or are you moving on?'

'I don't know,' I said. 'My goat ran off. What's out there?' I pointed in the direction that Nanny had gone.

'Not a lot,' the woman answered. 'The old Risby place and a couple of other farms. Not that you could call them farms now.' She began mixing flour and water in a dish. 'Do you want some flat bread?'

I nodded and asked the woman when Luca and his companion had left.

'Couple of days ago. They're travelling fast. Two on one horse and the pony frisky and bright-eyed. Don't ask me how. They were a strange pair. The man hardly spoke and the boy never shut up – said he was some sort of weatherman and he was going to bring the rains. He's asking for trouble, mouthing off like that.'

Two days! How could I ever catch up to them at that rate? They couldn't have stopped to sleep.

A man came into the kitchen, pulling on his shirt. He rubbed his eyes and yawned. 'You're talking about that kid,' he said. 'Well, I believed him. He had the look. He was tall and thin as a lightning rod.'

The man made coffee and as the smell drifted out of the kitchen I heard people stirring. The woman cooked the bread and dished me out some bacon. I'd just started eating when I heard someone yelling outside. A door slammed and a woman who looked a bit like Auntie Shirl appeared.

'Who owns the milch goat?' she shouted. 'A white one. Long ears and curly horns.'

'She's mine.'

The woman stood before me with her arms folded.

'You owe me for a broken shed door and half a dozen busted rails of a pen. That goat has caused a load of trouble.'

'Why? What happened?'

'The animal's a rogue. Just come and look.'

The angry woman turned and walked away. I left my breakfast and led Sol after her. We found ourselves heading towards a broken-down hut with a collection of sheds behind it.

'The only place for a goat like that is hanging in a meat safe.' The woman pointed to one of the sheds. 'See for yourself.'

I left Sol beside her and went to investigate. The door had been flattened and an iron bedstead was wired in its place. Nanny was inside and two tiny kids were with her. They were small and weak and only one of them was standing.

'Look what I found, Ellie. Aren't they adorable!' Nanny whispered.

She licked the kid that was lying down and then nudged it to its feet.

'Come on, kidling. Time for another feed.' The tiny goat took a few tottering steps. Nanny watched fondly while it sucked, and when its little tail began wagging, she murmured, 'That's it, my sweet, drink deep.

'Their mother has no milk,' she explained quietly. 'It was a wonder she survived the birth. Look at her, poor thing.'

An old brown doe was lying against the back wall of the shed behind the remains of a broken pen. She was watching the kids.

'I told her not to worry. I have plenty of milk and I'll look after them until she's on her feet again.'

'See the mess?' I heard the woman yell. 'You're not getting your goat back until you pay for the damage. And if you've got no money you can stay and work it off. Either that, or I'll accept the goat as payment.'

Nanny put her head against the gate. 'I'll stay. I'll catch you up later.'

I looked at her in disbelief. 'Nanny, you can't stay here,' I whispered.

'These kidlets need me. They need milk.'

'We have to catch up with Luca and get the button-box. We've got to take it back to where it came from. We haven't got time to be rearing baby goats. Nanny, are you out of your mind?'

'Calm down, Ellie. There's no point in throwing a tantrum.'

'It's not a tantrum. We can't stay.'

'You can't, but I can.'

Nanny turned and looked at the kids.

'I won't leave these little darlings,' she said. 'You'll have to go on alone.'

'But Nanny—' I begged.

'You've got the horse. That's some company. Be brave, my girl.'

'But Nanny, I need you.'

She gave me a gentle nudge. She was pushing me away. How could she! I'd lost everything – Oma, my home, and now I was losing her as well.

'No, Nanny, you can't,' I cried.

She nudged me harder and there was nothing to do but walk away.

'Are you working for me, or what?' the woman asked as I took Sol's reins.

I shook my head.

I rode back to the way-house, ate my breakfast and filled my saddlebags with oats. I would feed Sol later, as soon as I found a place to stop. I didn't want to stay in the way-house full of strangers.

I went along the road until I found a stand of ironwood trees. A few carts came past and then a straggly mob of cattle. They looked like I felt – lost and confused. They wandered this way and that across the road and if it wasn't for the man riding behind them, cracking his stockwhip, they might have turned back.

I sat in the shade and forced myself to look at the road ahead. I tried to put Nanny out of my mind and I didn't think of Oma either. Instead I thought about my real family. I imagined them waiting for me at Stolt. What was that boss man's name – Rush? As soon as I reached the cattle fair I'd seek him out.

I pictured my mother. She'd have thick hair and a round face like me. She'd take me into her herder's tent and once I'd showed her my foot she'd know me for her daughter. She'd put her arms around me and hold me close. And she'd swear we'd never lose each other again.

I took the charm Rye had made for me and wished with all my heart to find my true family.

22

The Road to Stolt

I FINISHED THE FLAPJACKS on that first day out from Slattern Creek. Nanny had told me not to speak to strangers but because I was hungry I spoke to people on the way. Sometimes they gave me food – beefstraps, hardtack, and once an apple that was so dried and wrinkled it looked like a shrunken head. The settlements were few and far between and the Trunk Road was relentless, hot and dusty in the daytime and bitterly cold at night. It bore due west, carrying me towards the cattle fair.

I began to lose track of time. Each day was much like the next. I mostly travelled at night, resting in the daytime. Each morning after sun-up I would find shelter and if there was no shade I would lie in Sol's shadow and wait out the heat of the day. Sometimes I woke in full sun, feeling dizzy and parched. I think my mind began playing tricks on me because one day I imagined Nanny was with me.

'How long have we been gone?' I asked her.

'Years, my dear,' she replied.

Was it heat stroke? How could she believe that? 'It can't be more than a month,' I said.

She was standing above me, trailing her beard across my face. She blinked and gave a little bleat. 'Ah meh! I thought you meant how long since we left home.'

'I did, Nanny.'

'It's years, believe me. Time flows differently there.'

The conversation didn't make sense.

That night the road stretched endlessly in both directions. I wished Nanny was with me. I missed her company and I also missed her milk. I was so hungry and tired, it was a struggle keeping upright in the saddle. Without Nanny to look out for me I couldn't afford to sleep. And I worried about Sol, travelling far with so little to eat and drink.

'Once we reach the Gleam country things will be different,' I told him. 'It's a land of plenty, a place of flowing streams and lush pasture. You'll be up to your fetlocks in clover and pools of cool water will well up under your hoofs.'

❧

I WAS RELIEVED to reach Hope Springs, which I learned was the last stop before Stolt. A man had set up a stall on the edge of the township selling food and drink, and because water was scarce, he was charging by the cup. I had no money left but I held out my milking mug. The man looked at Sol, checking his shoulder.

'No charge,' he said.

Once again it seemed that fellow – or maybe it was Luca – had paid my way.

'They'd be at the fair by now,' the man said. 'Felt a bit sorry for the kid. His brother doesn't treat him well.'

'His brother?'

'Brother, manager. Whatever he is.'

'I don't know why you'd think they were brothers. The fellow's old and Luca's just a boy.'

The man shrugged. 'There wouldn't be ten years between them,' he said as he dished me out a bowl of stew.

'How far's Stolt?' I asked.

'If you left now you'd be there by morning. The fair's already started. It's been going for a week.'

I sat out the heat of the day in the shadow of a building, then left in the late afternoon. By evening a dust cloud appeared on the horizon, the first sign of Stolt. When darkness came I fell asleep in the saddle under a blood red moon.

23

The Cattle Fair

I ARRIVED IN STOLT the next evening. I couldn't
see the town for the drovers' camps that surrounded
it – hundreds of tents and wagons parked on the out-
skirts. The air was thick with dust and woodsmoke
from cooking fires, and the whole place was crowded
and chaotic. It wasn't going to be easy finding Luca.
I kept my eye out for Stumpy's pony, but there were more
horses than I'd ever seen before. Dogs were barking,
people were arguing, and somewhere far ahead I could
hear the sounds of the sale taking place: bellowing
cattle, an auctioneer calling for bids and the buyers
shouting out their offers. I stopped at the first bit of free
ground I came across, but as soon as I dismounted
somebody yelled, 'Move on. That's where the cattle
come through.'

I kept going until the roadway opened out into an
area that held stockyards and the ring where the animals

were sold. It was dark by then and the sale had stopped for the day. The place smelt of heat and dust and cow dung, and I could hear the cattle bumping against the railings in the yards.

I stopped near the auctioneer's stand at the side of the ring. A ladder leaned against it, and I sat on the bottom rung and wondered what to do. There was no point searching for Luca in the dark. I'd have to wait until morning.

'Stay here, Sol. I won't be long.'

I knew Sol would do as I asked. I didn't have to worry that he'd be stolen either; he could get a mean look about him if he needed to, a look which scared people off. And he was so big and strong nobody could force him to move if he'd decided against it.

I headed off to find the boss man. The herders didn't look friendly. They sat in groups around their fires, drinking out of cow horns. Their dogs snarled at me as I passed. I heard fighting and laughter and sometimes singing, but there was no joy in the songs. I tried to gather my courage to ask after Rush. It wasn't just the dogs that frightened me, it was the people too. They had a restless air about them, not unlike the cattle trapped in the yards. I guess they longed to be on the open road and were stuck here in Stolt.

After some time I came to a campsite that was quieter than the others. The people were sitting with their dogs at their feet, roasting meat on a spit; the smell made my mouth water. I edged closer and stood just beyond the circle of light from their fire, listening.

'This fair's the end of droving on the plains,' an old man said.

'It's the end of droving everywhere. If it doesn't rain soon we won't be travelling anymore.'

'What will we do if the mob don't sell?' A woman with long grey hair and a scarf around her head tapped out her pipe on her boot heel.

'Let them loose. There's no point in taking them back.'

'It might all come right,' a boy said. 'That fellow's performing tomorrow. They say he's the real thing.'

The others laughed.

'If you believe that, you'll believe anything.' The old man spat into the fire.

'Nothing like a drought to bring out the fake rainmakers,' the woman said. 'I for one won't be getting up at dawn to see his act. I'm sick of hearing about it.'

My breath caught in my chest. Luca was here, close by – and so was the button-box!

Just then one of the dogs lifted its head and growled in my direction, and a man who was squatting by the fire peered into the dark.

'Who's there?'

As soon as he spoke the dog leapt up and snapped at me. I jumped back, my hands in front of my face. The man was on his feet in an instant. He grabbed my wrist and noticed the tattoo.

'A way-child,' he said. 'What're you up to?'

He pulled me forward and the woman with the scarf held up a lamp. I was too frightened to speak.

The woman's eyes were the same grey as her hair. 'Talk,' she demanded.

'...Rush.'

'Why do you want him?' The man gripped me tighter.

'I'll take her,' the woman said. 'She might be useful.' She grabbed my arm and led me away, holding the lantern before her.

We passed a row of horses tethered between two carts. Then the woman turned right and, sidestepping a heap of firewood, found a path that wound between the camps.

I began to realise that what looked like a random arrangement of tents, wagons and makeshift shelters was actually organised. Each camp was either roped off or guarded by dogs, and a network of pathways led from one to the other. I tried to keep track of the way we were going because I was getting further and further from Sol, but I was soon lost in the maze. The woman circled wide around a ring of wagons, then stopped at the entrance to a brushwood enclosure. A man barred our way.

'He's not hiring. How many more times do I have to say it?'

The woman held the lantern near her face.

'Ah, it's you, Nemie.' He led us into an area crowded with people. A big fire blazed in the centre and a rough shed stood on one side. It had gaps between the boards and a tarp roof. A bag hung over the door and a young fellow stood leaning against the door frame, rubbing grease into a bridle. The woman ducked her head under the bag, pulling me after her.

People sat against the walls and cow hides covered the floor. A man with deep lines around his mouth sat dealing cards, using an upturned feedbin for a table. His hands were gnarled and he had the same grey eyes as the woman.

'Found one,' she said. 'She's young and probably not skilled yet. You can see if she's any good.'

He looked me up and down then returned to his cards.

'This is Rush,' she told me.

I took a deep breath. Here he was, the man who could help me find my family – my ma and my pa. Maybe I even had a grandmother somewhere, a *real* grandmother.

I should have been pleased, but my legs trembled and my mouth was dry.

'Yes?' he said, without looking up.

When I didn't say anything he swept the cards aside. Somebody lifted me onto the feedbin and I gave a cry of fright.

Rush was sitting on a box. He leaned back and rested his boot on his knee.

'What do you want?'

'I'm looking for some herders. I don't know their names. They came—'

He held up his hand. 'Information comes at a cost.'

Rush had thin lips and they barely moved when he

spoke. He reminded me of a snake. 'If I help you, you'll help me. Is that a deal?' he asked.

I nodded, although I had no idea how I could help him.

'Go on,' he said, 'Tell me about the herders.'

'They came over the pass near my home. I . . . they . . .' I wanted to ask him outright if he knew the drovers who'd left me behind, but something made me cautious. '. . . they had a goat with them.'

'Where are you from?' he asked.

'Mt Ossa.'

I watched him closely. Did he know Mt Ossa?

'The northern drove, the uplands. Is there rain there?'

I shook my head, although I didn't see what rain had to do with it.

'A goat, you say? Jinx Roan once travelled with a goat. He left the roads years ago and bought land up near Plinth, in the middle country.'

There – I had a name! It might be the name of my father, and if it wasn't, he would know who my parents were. I had no idea where Plinth was and I'd never heard of the middle country, but I'd find out and go there. It looked as though finding my parents was going to be easier than I thought.

'Why do you want to know?' Rush asked.

'There was a baby . . . a baby left on the hillside.'

'Hold it right there.' He put his hands around my ankles. 'Herders never abandon their own. No herder would leave a baby on the trail.'

'Maybe the cattle stampeded. They might have thought it was trampled—' I pulled against his grip but he fixed me with a cold stare and held me tight.

'Now it's my turn.' He leaned forward, looking up at me through half-closed eyes. 'It's a sad day when herders are forced to ask a half-trained way-girl for directions,' he sighed. 'But I'll do it. Here's the problem, way-child. We've always followed a circuit. We never made up our own routes, but now, with the water going underground and the drinking holes all but dried up, the known trails are gone.' He spread his hands and gave a grim laugh. 'You could say we're lost. Do you know the water paths? Can you map them?'

I didn't reply. I knew I couldn't begin to map the water paths. I didn't even know what they were. But I could tell that he wasn't going to take no for an answer so I gave a nod.

'Are you hungry? Sit down. Rig, bring some food!'

I sat on the floor next to the feedbin. The young man from outside appeared with meat on a slab of bread. I hadn't eaten all day and I fell on it, letting the fat drip down my chin. Rush watched me steadily and only when I finished and wiped my hand across my mouth did he speak again.

'What do you need? Some use a willow twig and others draw straight into the sand. Rig!' He snapped his fingers and the fellow put his head through the door once more. 'Get a tray.'

I knew I had to get away before they found out I couldn't help them. Warily, I got to my feet as Rush came and stood before me. Then, I gathered up all my courage and kicked him hard in the shins. Rush opened his eyes wide for the first time. There was a moment's disbelief, then those thin lips parted and he let out a bellow of rage. I ducked out the door and ran, pushing through the crowd.

I was caught before I reached the gate. Rough hands dragged me back in front of Rush.

'You'll do as I ask,' he said.

'I can't. I don't know how.'

When I started crying he gazed at the roof and sighed. 'Water's short and you're wasting good salt tears. Do the map and you can leave.'

'I can't do it.'

'Put her in the cart,' he said. 'Don't let her out until she's ready to divine.'

The fellow whose name was Rig took me to a wagon that had high wooden sides and no roof. He locked me in and went away, returning with a flask of water, a tray full of sand and a rough blanket that smelt of horses. He looked over his shoulder and spoke quietly.

'You have luck on your side, way-child. I know Roan. I was on the route with him when I was a boy. The goat had spiral horns.'

'That's her!' I gasped. 'I was the baby.'

Rig looked at me closely. 'Yes, you could be. I was about twelve then, and now I'm twenty-four.'

He placed the tray in front of me and told me to get started.

'I don't know how to make the map.'

'Maybe it will come to you. Rush won't give up. He'll keep you here until you do it.'

I looked blankly at the sand.

'Is Roan my father?' I asked.

'Roan?' He seemed surprised and was about to answer when a woman with a long plait wound around her head arrived.

'The boss wants you, Rig. I'll mind the girl.' She turned to me. 'Don't try Rush's patience too long or we'll all suffer. Get down to it and do your work.'

The woman went outside and bolted the door. 'Call me when you're done,' she said.

24

The Way-girl

I CLOSED MY EYES, trying to picture a map of the water paths, but I had no idea what to do. I rolled myself in the blanket and lay down. I watched the moon travelling across the sky. What had Meridian said – 'Rest your mind and let the map make itself?' That didn't help. I hoped Sol was all right, left alone by the auctioneer's stand.

Eventually I drifted into an uneasy sleep that was full of the sounds of the herders' camp – voices, dogs barking, people fighting and singing. Then came a voice I recognised. It was Meridian.

'Who's the map for?' she asked.

'The snake,' I whispered, thinking of Rush.

'Then follow its path. That's my advice.'

I don't know whether I was awake or asleep when I poured the water on the sand and watched the way it ran. It trickled silver in the moonlight and soaked away, but I kept the pattern in my mind. Then I smoothed the surface until it was flat and shiny and I began again, using my finger to draw a long wriggling snake trail from east to west. It was like tracing one map on another and when I'd finished I sat back and saw the spots where the new line crossed the old. I marked each one with a star.

'There, it's done!' I said, and I knew it was true, although I worried that the sand would dry by morning and my map would disappear. I banged on the walls and yelled until the woman came and took the tray away.

***

IT WAS DAWN when Rig opened the door.

'You're free to go. I'll show you the way.'

He led me outside the enclosure and past the circle of wagons. There were many more people than when I'd arrived. They were all hurrying in the same direction.

'What's going on?' I asked.

'There's entertainment in the ring. Which way are you heading, girl? It's going to be hard to move against this crowd.'

'Where's Plinth?'

I didn't intend to go there immediately, but I thought I'd better ask while I had the chance.

Rig cut between two rows of tents, dodging guy ropes and piles of wood.

'There's no point in going to Plinth,' he said. 'Roan's not your father.'

Just then a group of people streamed past, nearly knocking me over. Rig yelled something I didn't hear.

'What did you say?' I struggled to catch up to him and when I did I found myself on a thoroughfare that might have been the same one I'd followed when I arrived.

'The baby wasn't Roan's.'

'Stand aside!' a man yelled as some riders came through. They raised a choking dust and Rig and I were separated. He shouted above the noise.

'That baby didn't belong to the herders. They were paid to deliver it.'

Another group of horses passed and more people followed in their wake.

'Deliver it? From where?'

I was pushed along and when I looked back he was far behind me.

'Whose baby was it?' I cried. 'Where did it come from? Who owned it?'

The crowd surged forward, carrying me away. When I looked back, Rig was lost in the throng.

⁂

I WAS SWEPT along the roadway and before long I saw the auctioneer's stand by the ring. Sol stood where I'd left him and, despite the crowds, there was a wagon-sized area of clear ground around him. His ears were back and he was tossing his head – people were keeping well away. He settled as soon as he heard my voice, and once I was beside him he let the crowd close in around us. I mounted so I could see what was going on.

Everyone was pressing towards the stand, a sea of heads, jostling and moving forwards. I'd never seen so many people. I closed my eyes and saw them swarming towards the centre of the fair like dust particles moving on a map. It gave me an uneasy feeling.

When I opened my eyes I saw the crowd part to let somebody through, a pushy fellow with sandy hair. He looked familiar. He brushed past me to climb the ladder, and with a start I recognised the coat. It was the frockcoat the man-without-dust had worn, or one very like it. Then I saw he was wearing the same pointy shoes. From the top of the stand he turned and surveyed the crowd.

'Welcome,' he cried. 'Today you'll witness something you'll never forget.'

There was no hint of a wheeze in his voice. If this was the same man, he was now young and strong. The coat was tight on him and his hair was no longer grey.

'Where's the rain-boy?' someone yelled.

'He'll be here at noon.'

A disappointed sigh rose from the audience and a heckler yelled, 'Stage fright, is it? Has he chickened out?'

The man waved the fellow away. 'Believe me, it'll be worth the wait. The boy's resting up. He's travelled far and he's got a way to go. After this performance we're heading into the border country, where the real desert begins.'

He looked over the crowd and I slipped off Sol and ducked down, hoping he hadn't noticed me.

'Pappy Storm was the greatest rainman that ever lived, and the Lightning Lad is his grandson. The boy will speak to the skies. By this afternoon you'll be dancing in the rain.'

A cheer rose from the crowd. Some people sat down as if the show was about to start. Others stood doubtfully with their arms folded.

'I'll believe it when I see it,' a lady near me said.

'Rain!' the sandy-haired fellow cried. 'Rain, rain, rain!'

Most of the audience took up the chant.

Another man climbed the ladder, a short fellow in a white shirt and necktie. He had a pencil behind his ear and he was carrying a mouth trumpet and notebook.

'Clear off. This is my stand.'

'It's the auctioneer,' somebody said. 'If he wants to sell cattle today he hasn't got a hope.'

The two men turned their backs on the crowd. They were having some sort of altercation and I took the opportunity to slip away and look for Luca.

People were still streaming towards the middle of the fair and Sol had to make his way through them, but once we got past the crowds the camps were clear. There was nobody about, just horses, carts, tents and firewood. I wasn't worried about the dogs now that I was on horseback. I began moving along the paths, looking for Stumpy's pony. She could be anywhere and I feared it would take me hours to find her. The paths branched this way and that and I often found myself passing the same wagon twice.

Then I remembered mapping the water paths. I closed my eyes and let go of the reins. *Let the map make itself*, I whispered. The lines I saw in my mind were like tangled twine but as I watched, one way became clearer than the others. It weaved towards the edge of the camps where the tents were not pitched so close together. When I opened my eyes, Sol was striding towards a little tent that stood by itself next to a stunted tree. He whinnied and a horse answered him. The mare was tethered some distance away. I slipped off Sol and ran towards the tent.

There was a showy sort of saddle on the ground outside. The leather was black and richly tooled and there were silver buckles on the stirrup straps. It was dusty but I could see it was new.

'Luca?'

There was no answer. The tent flaps were firmly laced up and the canvas sides were pegged down so tightly it took all my strength to loosen them so that I could stick my head under.

Luca was there, crouched against the far wall, his rope slung over his chest. He wore boots with fancy stitching and he'd exchanged his patched shirt for a brand new buckskin vest with a fringe. But for all that, he didn't look happy. His hair hung loose and he was hollow eyed. He stared at me in fright as I wriggled under the canvas. He held the button-box in his hands.

'Thief!' I grabbed the instrument but Luca wouldn't

let go. His face was white and he had a strange look in his eye.

'I'm shackled!' he cried.

When I tried to pull the button-box from him, he yelped in pain.

'The handstraps—' he gasped.

I let go and looked at Luca's hands. They were squashed beneath the straps and the leather was cutting into him.

'That fella...He tightened them.' His eyes darted to the tent flap and back to me.

'Where is he?' he breathed.

'He's on the stand, talking up your show.'

'No, he's not. He's not there. He's not anywhere,'

'What do you mean?'

Luca looked so wild eyed and desperate I wondered if he'd lost his wits.

'What's wrong with you?' I asked. 'What's happened?'

'Is Rye here? Did you come with Meridian?'

'I came by myself.'

Luca looked as if he might cry.

'He's got me, Ellie. I'm his, like the button-box.'

'What are you talking about?'

'At first he seemed helpful...he said he'd be my manager...all I had to do was play for him. But the more I played, the worse it got. And the last time...' Luca looked at his hands in desperation. 'It was near Hope Springs and I'd had enough...It was horrible, Ellie. I wanted to stop but I couldn't. I would have dropped the thing but he stared at the straps with his weird eye and they became tighter as I played.'

There was cheering in the distance and the crowd began chanting again: *Rain, rain, rain!*

'Get the weather-boy!' someone shouted. 'Bring him now!'

Luca rocked on his heels, his hands held tight.

'Help me,' he said. 'Get it off.'

'What with?' There were no buckles on the hand-straps. They were sewn onto metal rings. I'd need a knife to cut the leather. I looked around the tent. There was nothing in it except a blanket and my gunny sack.

Outside, there was a shrill whistle and then hoof-beats, coming closer.

'Over here!' somebody yelled.

I heard footsteps outside the tent and before I could do anything the tent flaps were torn open and a mob burst in, whooping and cheering. They grabbed Luca and hauled him outside. Then he was hoisted up in the air and carried off. He looked more like a prisoner on his way to the gallows than a young rainmaker about to give his first performance.

I mounted Sol and followed in his wake. When he reached the stand a great roar rose from the audience. The man in the frockcoat was waiting at the top of the ladder and the auctioneer was with him. They seemed to have worked out their differences because the auctioneer helped Luca up.

'Here he is, ladies and gentlemen, Luca the Lightning Lad, grandson of the great Pappy Storm.'

The auctioneer's voice crackled through the mouth trumpet.

'This is your moment, boy,' the man in the frockcoat said.

Standing at the top of the ladder like that, Luca looked so tall he almost reached the sky. He stared at his feet, his shoulders hunched and his knees slightly bent as if he was trying to make himself smaller.

I urged Sol onwards, pushing my way through the crowd. If people were trodden underfoot it couldn't be helped. Luca was without his rubber boots and he was the highest point around. Suddenly I saw lightning in my mind.

'Get down from there!' I yelled.

I don't think he heard me.

A hush fell over the crowd, all eyes on Luca.

I don't know what they expected him to do, but he did nothing – he just kept staring at his feet, shaking like a leaf. The auctioneer quickly filled the waiting silence.

'Talk is cheap, ladies and gentlemen, but rain is precious. Give the boy some encouragement.'

Someone passed him a battered tin dish like the ones prospectors use for panning gold. He held it out. 'Let's have a show of confidence!'

People went through their pockets, throwing in coins, and when the auctioneer held the trumpet close, the sound was like rain on a tin roof.

'That's the way, give generously. Your investment will be rewarded a hundredfold.'

He waited until the dish was full, then said, '*Now* let's see what the lad can do.'

I was nearly at the stand when the fellow in the frockcoat noticed me. He gave a wave, then turned his attention to Luca.

'Play,' he said. 'Play for me!'

He whispered something to the auctioneer, who went over and released the catch on the button-box. It immediately sprang open and Luca began to play, his eyes wide with fright and his mouth set in a painful grimace. There was no sound, of course, but I felt the change in the air. Everyone did. The temperature immediately dropped and clouds appeared from the southwest; they looked like lumps of grey, felted fleece. The day darkened. The cattle in the yards grew restless and the trampling of their hoofs merged with the sound of distant thunder.

'He's doing it!' a lady yelled. 'He's pulling in a storm!'

The auctioneer stared at the horizon. The sky began to shake and flash, lighting the yards and the roofs of the town beyond. He took the dish and quickly disappeared down the ladder.

Luca stood frozen to the spot, staring at the sky. His long hair began to rise. It fanned out around his face until it stood on end.

'Luca, get down!' I screamed.

When Sol reached the stand I jumped onto the ladder, climbing as fast as I could. A woman tried to pull me back.

'What are you doing? Don't you want the drought to break?'

'Luca, jump!'

This time he heard me. He looked down and it was as if he woke from a trance.

I scrambled back onto my horse and Luca half jumped, half fell down the ladder. I caught hold of the rope across his chest and pulled him onto Sol, in front of me. There was a blinding flash of lightning and chaos followed. People shrieked, horses bolted and there was the sound of splitting timber as one of the yard rails gave way and cattle broke free, stampeding through the crowd.

I rode hard towards a lane that ran behind the yards, one arm holding Luca and the other holding the reins. The button-box was still playing. As soon as we got clear of Stolt I put both hands on the instrument.

'Push it shut,' I yelled. 'Push it with all your strength.'

Luca did as I asked and I managed to slip the catch. At once the instrument was still. Luca slumped back, exhausted.

'Get it off me,' he breathed.

'I will, but not here.'

We had a head start, but I knew the man on the stand – the man-without-dust – wouldn't be far behind us.

PART FOUR

25

The Dugout

I DIDN'T TAKE any notice of the direction we went. I just wanted to get far away from the cattle fair. That fellow would have to go back for the pony and it'd be hard for him to make his way through the crowds. The lightning had stopped and the dark clouds were rolling away to the east. There was no rain. I imagined the excitement of the mob would soon turn to anger. Perhaps people would stop him leaving Stolt. They might grab him and the auctioneer and demand their money back. I crossed my fingers and leaned forward in the saddle as Sol galloped on.

We found ourselves on a back road beyond the town. There were low hills and a few rocky outcrops ahead, and when we crested a rise I saw a farmhouse.

'I'll get help,' I told Luca.

He was weak and shaky, but he managed to get off Sol and follow me to the door.

There was nobody around – they were probably at the fair. I knocked, and when there was no answer I pushed the door open and went in.

Luca sat down at the kitchen table with his arms stretched before him while I examined the handstraps of the button-box. The leather was cracked, and once I found a bread knife it was easy to saw through it. I pulled both straps free of the metal rings that held them in place. As soon as Luca was released he backed away and leaned against the kitchen bench, rubbing his wrists and staring at the instrument as if he feared it might come after him. Then, with a sigh, he slid to the floor. He was trembling all over and his face was bone white.

'It's his, you see,' Luca said. 'He made it and he wants it back.'

'Who is he?'

'I don't know. He said he wanted to help me use my gift. He told me he'd seen my grandpappy perform. What a fool I was to believe him. It's all lies.'

He rubbed his hands and flexed his fingers, getting back the circulation.

'He made me play it every night, all the way from Horseshoe Bend. The worst of it was that each time I played that thing, he got stronger.'

Luca looked towards the door as if he feared some-one might hear.

'He reckoned the music did him good. It made him lively. But it was more than that. It was like food for him.'

Luca wasn't making much sense.

There was a water pot by the back door with a dipper hanging off it. I gave him a drink and went through the cupboards looking for something to eat. When I found some bread I figured the owners wouldn't mind sharing it.

'If he wanted the button-box, why didn't he take it?' I asked.

'I don't think he could.'

I broke off a hunk of bread and handed it to Luca.

'That fella didn't eat. That was the first thing I noticed. Not one thing, all the way to Stolt. He didn't drink either, and I never saw him sleep. I'd wake in the night and he'd be sitting there watching me. It gave me the screaming jitters.'

He shoved the bread in his mouth. 'He never held anything. Not once did he saddle the pony, and when he tightened those straps on me he didn't do it with his hands, he just stared at the button-box and I was bound. I think he's a haint.'

'A ghost?' It was hard to believe.

'He's some sort of spook. I watched him day after day and no matter where the sun was, he never cast a shadow.'

My head was aching as I tried to make sense of this.

'People told me he paid for my food and board. How did he do it?'

'He made me hand over the coins.'

'Why was he paying for me? I don't even know him.'

'Well, he knows you. He never stopped looking over

his shoulder. When we reached Stolt he was waiting for you to catch up.'

I stared at Luca in bewilderment. The only thing I knew for sure was that we'd better get going, because I felt that fellow on my trail even as Luca spoke.

When I picked up the button-box he looked alarmed.

'Let's go,' I said.

'Leave it. Put it down.'

'I need it. Come on. We can't sit here waiting for him.'

⁕

THE TRAIL LED into some hills beyond the farm and after a time it narrowed and became no more than a goat track. I kept looking back but we weren't being followed. Not yet.

By noon we needed shade. When the path forked I let Sol choose the way, and he found the perfect shelter – a dugout, or maybe the entrance to an old mine. It was built into the side of a hill and the opening was big enough for a horse. Inside it was dark and cool and looking out we'd be able to see someone coming from a long way off.

'That fellow wasn't lying about your gift,' I said as I got off Sol. 'Look what happened at Stolt.'

'That was the button-box, not me.'

'It was you. You have the gift. Rye told me.'

Luca slid to the ground. 'He didn't tell me!'

'He was trying to protect you, and so was Meridian.

That's why she made you wear those rubber boots. To keep you safe.'

We drank from the waterbag then sat with our backs against the wall.

'Safe from what?' Luca asked.

'Lightning. Do you know what happened to your mother?'

'She died in an accident when I was small. She was hit by a wagon.'

'It wasn't a wagon that hit her. It was lightning. You were there and the lighting came for you just like it did today. Your father was holding you above his head. He handed you a sky rod and you would have been killed but your mother took it from you. That's how she got struck.'

I could see it in front of my eyes. 'She saved you, Luca, and so did Rye and Meridian.'

Luca was quiet for a while. When he spoke he might have been talking to himself.

'There's things I remember. When I was little my fingers would tingle when I looked at the sky. The hairs on my arm would rise when a storm was brewing. I could always feel them coming. I could smell rain before it arrived and sometimes, when I slept, my dreams were full of thunder. Then it all faded. It passed over like the weather.'

He put his head in his hands. After a while I realised he was weeping. Was he crying for his mother?

'You couldn't help it, Luca. You were only a baby.'

'I'm not crying for the past,' he whispered.

'What then?'

'For the future. For a life spent in fear, wearing safety boots and crouching under the sky.'

He gave a deep sigh and wiped his eyes on his sleeve. Then he stared out across the parched land.

'You don't know that,' I said. 'It might all change.'

He looked at me doubtfully, and something about him reminded me of Tod. He was older than me but he seemed small and lost.

'Could you do me a map, Ellie?' he asked. 'Did Meridian teach you?'

'I can try, but not now.'

There was a horse in the distance.

'Move away from the entrance,' I said.

Luca scrambled behind me. 'We should go. Get away now while there's time.'

'He'll see us leave. Better to stay out of sight.'

I led Sol some way into the dark. I couldn't tell how far the dugout went into the hill, but it was easy to feel my way along. Then I left him and went back to the entrance, pressing myself against the wall as I peered out.

The rider tracked towards us. I was too far away to see if it was Stumpy's pony, but I expect it was. When he reached the fork in the trail he paused and stared at the ground. I tried to remember if the path down there was soft or stony. I hoped Sol hadn't left hoofprints.

It occurred to me that the-man-without dust might sense where the button-box was. I remembered how he'd stared at the closed cupboard in the way-wagon after

Meridian hid it there. As soon as I had that thought he looked up and gazed in my direction. My heart missed a beat. But the next moment he looked away. When he took the fork that headed west I heaved a sigh of relief. We watched until the horse was a tiny speck in the distance.

By then it was late afternoon.

'Now we can go back to Stolt and take the Trunk Road east,' Luca said.

'I'm not going east. I'm going west.'

Luca stared at me as if I was mad. 'You want to follow him?'

'I've got to take this button-box back to where it came from.'

I wasn't in a hurry to leave the dugout. I wanted to let that horse get far ahead. I watched the sun go down and as the stars came out I told Luca everything that had happened to me from the day of Pop's funeral until now.

'The button-box caused the crops to fail and it ruined the land, but worst of all was what it did to Oma. It was terrible to see and I knew it was all my fault. If there's truth in what she told me – that once the button-box is destroyed everything will come right – I have to try.'

Luca listened in silence. I told him about my auntie Shirl and my bad luck foot and how I'd learned that I wasn't part of the family and when there was nothing more to say, he stood up and went outside.

'Lights,' he said. 'I can see Stolt.'

He came back and sat down next to me.

'You can't go by yourself. I'll come with you.'

We decided to leave early the next morning.

⚬⚭⚬

THAT NIGHT I DREAMED about Luca. In the dream he was almost a man, so I knew it was the future. He wasn't crouching under the sky wearing rubber boots. He was standing on top of a mountain, working the weather. He twirled one hand above his head as if he was swinging a rope, and the clouds came low and swirled around him. He banged his fists and made the sound of distant thunder. He put his palms together and reached for the sky, and the heavens split with a deafening crack. It was a language of signals and he moved smoothly from one sign to the next. It was like a dance.

I watched, mesmerised, as he drew lightning from the sky. When he showed the flat of his hand the lightning bolt flashed sideways, striking the ground nearby. I watched him flick his fingers, releasing a shower of rain, and I thought that I must remember each and every movement so I could tell Luca when I woke up. But then the dream changed and I saw that it wasn't Luca, but someone like him.

The fellow made circles in the air. He stirred the winds and dust blew in my eyes. When I looked again he was ancient: an old-time weatherworker. He nodded, gave a little bow, and opened a black umbrella painted with the words Pappy Storm. He smiled as the rain pattered down. The sound was loud in my ears.

I opened my eyes. There was no rain outside and the only light in the dugout was the faint glow that came from the moon mark on Sol's shoulder. I could still hear the pattering although I was wide awake. I sat up and woke Luca.

'Hear that?'

It was getting louder. I stuck my head out the entrance but there was definitely no rain about. I realised the sound was coming from behind me; it was coming from somewhere deep inside the hill. I thought I heard a baby cry. It was far away, but it echoed through the dugout. Before long I heard a familiar voice. 'Keep up, my dears. It's not much further.'

I realised it wasn't the patter of rain I was hearing but the patter of hoofs, goats' hoofs. A few minutes later Nanny Gitto appeared from the darkness. The old doe from Slattern Creek was behind her and so were the kids.

'There!' she said. 'I told you it wasn't far.'

26

The Underways

'NANNY, I THOUGHT I'd never see you again!'
I rushed towards her but she brushed me aside and
stood panting, staring at Luca then at the saddlebags.

'Have you got it back then?' she asked.

When I nodded she shuddered. 'Get rid of it,' she
said. 'It's got a bad history.'

'I know. Oma told me everything.'

'Your Oma doesn't know half of it. But I do. It's
been coming to me, night after night. I've hardly slept.'

The kids trotted up and sniffed me. They looked
tired but they were strong and sleek. Nanny began feeding them, one on each side, and the old doe sat down
with a weary sigh.

'I came to warn you,' Nanny said.

'Warn me about what?'

She lowered her voice. 'I can't speak in front of the
kids.'

The young goats were down on their knees, butting to make the milk flow faster.

'How did you find me?' I asked.

'I took a short cut through the underways. I'd forgotten they were there. I would have stayed until the kids were weaned but there wasn't time.'

Luca looked bewildered. It was obvious he couldn't hear Nanny.

When they'd finished feeding, the kids lay down beside their mother and went to sleep.

'Now we can talk,' Nanny said, leaning close. 'That story is getting stronger. You know I told you how that fellow Harland made Gola a gift?'

I nodded.

'It looked like a jewel box.' She glanced again at my saddlebags. 'But it wasn't a jewel box. It was a concertina.'

'What?'

'He used the materials he had at hand – goat hide for the bellows and bone for the buttons.'

I was feeling very strange and I didn't know if I wanted to hear any more.

'You understand why I didn't want to speak in front of the kids,' she whispered. 'This story would give them nightmares.'

'It will give *me* nightmares.'

Luca was looking at me as if he thought I'd gone mad. 'What will give you nightmares?' he asked.

'The goat girl refused the gift along with all the others,' Nanny said. 'Then Harland came up with a plan. He practised playing the button-box until he made a tune that was so sweet even the wild creatures came at the sound: a tune that no human could resist.'

'What's going on?' Luca asked. 'Why are you talking to the goat?'

Nanny flicked her ears in annoyance. She was speaking fast and low. 'Ilk knew what he was up to. She heard him practising and she felt the pull of that strange music. Immediately she stopped up her daughter's ears with beeswax. She blocked her own as well, and took the girl to a faraway place where she could hear nothing but the wind blowing through the mountain peaks.'

'Ilk? Did you say Ilk?' I cried.

Nanny stamped her foot. 'Don't interrupt, Ellie. Listen to what I'm telling you.'

'But Ilk was the cure-all Oma told me about, the one who—'

'Ilk was Gola's mother.' Nanny's stare was fierce and I fell silent. She took a deep breath and went on.

'Gola worried about her friend Gabe. Every day she called to the goats – hers, and the wild goats that lived in the high country. *Yidda, yidda, yidda!* she called, and the goats came, but none of them had a red thread. She pined for Gabe and her belly grew round as the moon. She was expecting a child and she believed Gabe was the father.'

'Ellie, what's happening?' Luca asked, baffled.

'She's talking to me, Luca. She knows about that fellow. His name is Harland. Go on, Nanny.'

Nanny closed her eyes. She spoke so softly that I could barely hear her.

'He was furious that his plan to lure Gola had failed, and he put that fury into the instrument. He opened the button-box and buried his rage inside it, then he played long and hard and the music cursed the land and all who lived there – the people, the creatures and the plants. Gola's little baby lived and so did Ilk, but Gola didn't survive. She became thin and weak. Within a short time she had faded away to nothing. Then one night she went to sleep and didn't wake up. It was the same with the goats. Within a few weeks most of the herd had died.'

Nanny gave a little groan.

'It's just a story, Nanny. It's all in the past,' I said.

'The past is not over, Ellie. It's only just beginning. You shouldn't be carrying that thing. It's dangerous. I want you to get rid of it right now.'

'I can't. I'm taking it to the Palisades.'

'What did she say?' Luca looked from Nanny to me and back again.

'She thinks I shouldn't go on. The button-box is too dangerous and so is Harland.'

I didn't sleep that night and neither did Luca. The little goats were restless. They woke Nanny several times for a feed and I listened to them scuffling as they settled themselves back down beside their mother. We lay awake waiting for dawn.

WHEN THE SKY grew light I went outside and looked towards the west. There was no chance of me turning back. Oma had said that Alma West believed the button-box would find its end in the place where it began. If I didn't hold true and take it there, Oma would die and this journey would be for nothing. I realised I wasn't angry with my grandmother anymore – I'd left that behind somewhere along the Trunk Road. There was only one thing on my mind now, and that was destroying the button-box.

I fixed my eyes on the horizon, and as the sun came up a wall of bright mountains appeared in the west. They seemed impossibly close, their sheer stone cliffs rearing against the sky. They weren't there yesterday.

'Look, Luca!' I cried.

He stared where I pointed but he couldn't see any mountains. Nanny could, though.

'That's them,' she said. 'The Palisades. They're not the sort of mountains you can climb. Even a mountain goat would have trouble getting over them.'

'Then we'll go underground,' I said, remembering the tunnels I used to see when I was small. I closed my eyes and pictured them. Then I went to the entrance and looked into the darkness at the rear of the dugout. 'This way.' I felt sure the passage would take us to our destination.

⚬⚬⚬

'YOU'RE MULE-STUBBORN, Ellie West,' Nanny muttered as we made our way through the tunnel. Luca and I rode Sol and our legs scraped the rock wall.

I hoped it wasn't going to get any narrower, because if it did we'd have to leave Sol behind or find another way. The kids skittered ahead, refreshed after their sleep and an early morning feed. Their mother walked after them with her head down.

It was cool in the tunnel and the further we went the cooler it became. I took out my shawl and put it around both of us. When the passage widened and we could trot, the fabric flowed out behind us and seemed to give out light – or perhaps it was only reflecting the walls. The stone around us was pale, not red like the rocks outside and it shone as we passed. I wondered if it was moonstone, like Auntie Lil's necklace.

We reached a place where the tunnel branched. Nanny stopped and looked over her shoulder, refusing to go any further.

'Leave the button-box here, Ellie. We're turning back.'

'No, Nanny, we're going on.'

I sent my mind ahead of me and felt it pass under the wall of mountains. I had no idea how far we were underground, but it felt very deep, deeper than any miner would dig.

I started off again and Nanny reluctantly followed. When the passage opened into a cavern and Sol splashed through a creek, I knew these underways had been made by water. I remembered the map I'd drawn for the herders.

We stopped to drink and the water was clear and sweet. We continued, passing through the cavern and into another passage.

'Follow the flow path,' I told Nanny.

She trailed along behind. 'I think this is a mistake,' she said.

The path sloped downwards, gently at first, and then the way grew so steep that I had to lean back and hold the saddle horn as Sol lowered his head and slid down on his haunches. His hoofs scrabbled on the stone floor and occasionally he scattered a few pebbles; I heard the echo as they bounced ahead of us.

After some time the passage levelled out and Nanny stopped to feed the kids. I wondered how she could keep producing milk when she was hardly eating.

'I'm wondering too,' she said. 'If I was back on Spit Farm I'm sure I would have dried up by now.'

The thought of Spit Farm made my stomach clench. I hoped they hadn't run out of supplies and I hoped, if there was food, that Oma was still able to eat. When I pictured her lying on our palliasse my eyes filled with tears.

'I'm hungry,' Luca said.

'Get your mug, Ellie,' Nanny muttered. 'I can't spare much, but you and the boy should have a mouthful.'

When the kids had finished their feed I squeezed the last of the milk out of Nanny's teats and Luca and I shared it. I was hungry too, but I tried to put it out of my mind.

'How far do you think it is to those mountains you saw?' Luca asked.

'It looked to me like less than half a day's ride,' I said, but I wasn't sure.

As we travelled on, the old doe began to weaken. Nanny suggested she ride with me and I had a hard time balancing her in front of the saddle. By mid-afternoon I was weak with hunger and very tired. I tried to remember when I last ate. Apart from the piece of bread at the farmhouse, it must have been at the herders' camp.

The tunnel sloped steeply downhill and I couldn't manage the goat. She slipped awkwardly to the ground and I fell off trying to hold her. I knew I couldn't lift her back onto Sol so I walked beside him. When the passage climbed again I pushed the doe along in front of me. We walked for ages before Nanny called a halt.

'We'll sleep here,' she said as she nuzzled the kids.

I had no idea what time it was. The rocks gave out a soft, twilight gleam. There was a pool ahead of us and I heard the sound of water dripping from the rocks above.

Horses normally lock their knees and sleep standing up, but Sol lay down that night. When I leaned against his shoulder he rested his nose on my knee.

'It's all right, Sol. We'll be there by tomorrow. I'm sure of it.'

'I'm not,' said Luca. 'I don't think you know where you're going.'

'Yes I do – I told you. We're going under the Palisades.'

'They probably don't even exist.'

'Of course they exist. I saw them. And I know the Gleam land is on the other side.'

He sat leaning against the wall. 'This is madness,

Ellie. What will you do when we get there, *if* we get there?'

'Quiet, Luca. We need to rest. I'll know what to do in the morning.'

'It could be morning now for all you know. We can't go on without food. I think we should turn around. Do you know the way back?'

'Of course I do. Go to sleep,' I told him.

I closed my eyes and tried to retrace my steps, but everything looked different going backwards. One moment the passage was as wide as a wagon and the next it was impossibly narrow. The tunnels seemed to branch more often than I remembered, and as Sol left no hoofprints on the stone floor there was no way of knowing which route we had taken.

⁂

THE NEXT DAY the passage continued uphill.

'See, I told you,' I said. 'We'll surface before long and see the light of day.'

I was wrong. The passage dipped, winding its way down, and I lost all sense of direction. When we left the dugout I had felt we were heading west, but now we could have been going east or south and I had no idea if it was day or night. My belly groaned with hunger.

The kids began to tire and Nanny nudged them towards Sol.

'You'll have to carry them,' she said. 'Take one each.'

By evening – if you could call it evening – Luca and

I were exhausted. As we settled for our rest, I was beginning to think he was right – we should turn back. But by then I was completely lost.

'I wish you'd listened to me,' Nanny said. 'But it's too late now.'

She lay on the rock floor and we stretched out beside her.

'I can see why you didn't make me a map,' Luca said. 'There'd be nothing on it.'

'What do you mean?'

'No future, nothing ahead.'

'That's not true, Luca. I had a dream for you. I saw your grandpa. He was working the weather. He used his hands. That's how he did it. He made signals to the sky. Like this.'

I slowly twirled my hand above my head then I tried to remember what else I'd seen in the dream.

'He might have flicked his wrists,' I muttered. 'There was a sequence, one thing followed the next but I'm too tired now to think exactly how it went.'

Luca stared at the rocks above. 'It hardly matters,' he whispered.

FROM THEN ON, Luca barely spoke and neither did I. We didn't have the strength. The next time we stopped to rest I fell into a deep and dreamless sleep.

It might have been the middle of the night when Sol nudged me awake. Luca was leaning over my saddlebags.

I sat up with a start. 'What are you doing?'

He took out the button-box and placed it beside him. Then he picked up one of the saddlebags and shook it. A couple of Pop's sunflower seeds fell out.

'We've got to eat, Ellie.'

'One each,' I said.

He shook his head and poked the seeds into a patch of dust on the ground.

'I'm going to play the button-box.'

When he reached for the instrument I didn't try to stop him. I knew it was risky but I was so hungry that I could see those plants growing in my mind. I saw them bud and burst into flower, each bloom heavy with seeds, enough to fill our empty bellies.

He undid the catch but nothing happened. Without the handstraps he couldn't hold the instrument properly. He thought for a while, then took his rope and, finding a sharp rock in the wall, sawed off a length. He unravelled the strands so they'd fit through the little metal rings that had held the handstraps. He tied them off.

I held my breath as he slipped his hands under the rope.

Oma had told me that the button-box can give, but it can also take away. It didn't give us any food that night. And what it took was Luca.

The bellows sprang open and the buttons moved fast. The instrument rose into the air by itself, pulling Luca to his feet and away down the tunnel. I ran to grab his wrists and was dragged along with him.

Luca screamed as the button-box gathered speed.

Pop's hat fell off my head and the cold air rushed past my ears. I held on for as long as I could, but when the button-box swerved around a corner I lost my grip.

'I'll get my horse!' I yelled.

By the time I was on Sol, Luca's cries were far away, echoing through the underground. I galloped after him but he was moving impossibly fast. When Sol stopped I slid to the ground and put head in my hands.

Nanny came running and the other goats were behind her. She had Pop's hat in her mouth; she dropped it in front of me and stood panting, waiting for me to recover. I didn't have the strength to climb back on Sol.

'Take one of my horns,' she said, lowering her head.

Nanny took my weight and pulled me up. I leaned against her as we moved through the moonstone tunnels. One passage branched into the next and there was no way of knowing which way Luca had gone. I closed my eyes but I saw nothing except Luca's stricken face as he was carried away, his arms stretched before him and his long hair streaming behind.

27

The Palisades

AFTER SOME TIME the tunnel we were in began to climb. Nanny quickened her pace. She was surprisingly strong and she seemed to get stronger the further we went.

Then, when we had travelled for many hours, it wasn't the light of day we met, but the light of a lantern. It gleamed off the moonstone and threw long shadows on the floor.

'Halt!'

I was half asleep, my hands locked around Nanny's horn.

An old woman stood before us, blocking our way. She looked like a bundle of bones tied up in rags and she was brandishing a stick. Her hair was long and unkempt and there were things caught in it, twigs and leaves. It fanned out silver in the light. Her eyes were milky and they frightened me, so I stared at her feet, which were bare and knobbly.

She stepped towards us, holding up the lantern. When Nanny skittered away, I lost my grip and stood leaning against the rock wall.

The woman lifted my hat and looked at my face. Then she stared at my shawl. 'Who are you?' she demanded. Her voice was croaky and it frightened me almost more than the look of her.

'Ellie.'

'I don't care what name you go by. Tell me who you are.'

She waited for an answer. When I gave none, she brushed past me and looked at Sol's shoulder. She put her hand on his moon mark.

'Shine mount!' she declared. 'How did you come by him?'

'He belonged to my pop,' I whispered. 'He was handed down in the family.'

'What family?'

'My family.' I began to cry. I'd lost Luca. Oma could be dead by now and I was so tired I could hardly stand up. But I knew one thing – Oma and Pop and Tod and the others were still who I thought of when I said that word.

'My family,' I said again. 'This horse belongs to my family.'

Then the woman turned around and gazed at Nanny. Nanny stood her ground, her front feet wide apart and her great horns reaching skywards. She stared at the woman and the woman stared back. There was a long silence.

'Galita?' The old lady gasped. 'No...it can't be!'

'But it is,' Nanny said.

The lady peered again at my shawl. I was shocked when she fell to her knees in front of me and I found myself looking into her tangly grey hair. She began unlacing my boot, the boot to my wrong foot.

'Don't!' I cried, pulling away. 'What are you doing?'

She looked up, confused. 'I'm mistaken?' she asked. 'You're not her?'

Nanny stepped forward. I thought she was going to comfort me but she went to the lady and stood close. 'You're not mistaken,' she said quietly. 'We're back.'

The woman reached out and held Nanny's face in her hands. 'I always hoped one day I might see you again, Galita. And you...'

She struggled to her feet and hovered before me. I thought she was going to fall and when I put my hands out to stop her she clasped them and looked deep into my eyes.

'Why did you come?' she asked. 'It's not safe for you.'

'She came to bring the button-box,' Nanny said.

'It's here?' The old lady's eyes grew wide. 'Why? Why did you bring it?'

Her voice seemed to waver and fade. Nanny said something I couldn't hear. She sounded faint and far away. '...boy...tunnels...' I could make out some words but not others. I felt weak and dizzy and I began to slide down the wall. 'Harland,' someone said. I don't know if it was Nanny or the old woman.

'Harland's a ghost,' I muttered as I sank to the ground.

The lady was suddenly talking in my ear. 'A ghost is the image of someone dead. Harland is *alive*.'

Those were the last words I heard. I was vaguely aware of moving along the tunnel with Nanny on one side of me and the old lady on the other. I could feel her bony arm under mine.

❧

IT WAS A WHILE before I began to hear again. I wasn't sure if I was awake or asleep. Someone was feeding me with a spoon. I tasted oatmeal and honey.

'There are no goats left, Galita. Even the wild ones are gone. I've lost my power and I've almost lost my wits.'

'Not all of them,' Nanny said. 'Could you still make curd?'

'With what? I have no goats and no milk.'

'I have milk.'

The conversation was like something in a dream.

'Do you remember this place, Galita? It used to be the goat cave.'

'It seems a lifetime ago.'

'It was a lifetime. It was many lifetimes.'

I swallowed the oatmeal. 'That's it, my child — eat up.'

I became aware of the ground beneath me. It wasn't hard stone. It was something soft.

'Rest now,' the old lady said.

Sometime later I heard the sound of milk squirting into a bucket and when I opened my eyes I was lying on a thick felt mat looking up at the stone roof of a cavern.

I smelt smoke and lifted my head. The old woman was sitting by a fire, stirring a pot. Nanny was with her. Sol and the other goats stood some distance away, watching, and beyond them I could see the night sky through a narrow opening. The stars were bright and cool air blew over my face.

'It's boiled,' the lady said. 'Now we must let it set.'

She took the pot from the fire and covered it with a shawl that looked a lot like mine. 'There's no guarantee it will work, but it may still be potent. If I can cure myself I'll know what to do.'

They both gazed at the pot.

'I haven't made curd for a long time. The last person who ate my curd was someone from the world. Do you remember, Galita?'

Nanny shook her head. 'I've forgotten so much. How long will it take?' She sniffed the pot.

'I don't know. I used to know many things and now I hardly know my own name.'

By the wall of the cave there were some old feedbins and a rough-made shelf, which held a milking mug and an ancient wooden pail. Under the shelf was a neat pile of sticks, a blanket, a spindle and a string bag full of wool.

Nanny shook her wattles. 'I fear for the boy,' she said.

'It's not the boy that Harland wants,' the old lady muttered.

I let my head fall back and took a deep breath. When I next looked up, one of the kids was a few yards away, nibbling on my boot. I sat up with a start and made a grab for it. The kid dropped it in surprise.

'You're awake.'

The old woman picked up my boot and staggered towards me. I watched her put it back on my foot.

'I had to be sure,' she said, as she did up the laces. 'How are you feeling? Are you ill, or just exhausted?'

'She's just worn out,' Nanny said. 'Ellie's as tough as goats' knees.'

'The curd will help you,' the woman said. 'It will help all of us.'

'Who are you?' I asked.

She looked to Nanny.

'What have you told her, Galita?'

'Only what's come to me. At first it seemed like a story, a tale from long ago.'

'It *is* from long ago,' the old lady said. 'Time flows differently here. Did you tell her about the button-box?'

'Some,' Nanny said. 'I don't know myself what happened after he played that bad music.'

The lady left me and went back to the fire. She lifted the shawl and stirred the pot with a stick.

'My daughter was lost,' she said, 'and so were many like her.'

I had no idea who she was talking about.

'Gola,' Nanny said to me. 'Gola the goat girl was her daughter.'

The old woman coughed and hawked up a gob of spit. Then she went on talking, her voice dry and whispery.

'I took the baby and went at night to Harland's camp. I stole the instrument before more harm could be done, not realising that the worst had already happened. He came after me and I hid out near the Palisades. I cured a woman there – someone from beyond the mountains – and when she left I asked her to take the button-box away.

'After that, more people were failing every day. I could have helped them but the goats were failing too, and what little milk they gave I needed for the baby. I had none to spare for curd.'

She dipped her finger in the pot and tasted it.

'Surely you remember, Galita? Soon there was just the three of us – you, me and the baby, hiding out in the back country. And although Harland was blighted by the music the same as we were, he kept looking for me. He wanted Gola's child.'

I stared at her blankly. I didn't see what any of this had to do with me.

'I know it's hard to understand,' she said softly. 'I don't even know what to call you. You never had your naming day so I'll use the name your grandmother gave you, your *other* grandmother.'

I didn't know what she meant by that. I looked to Nanny and back again then I waited for the old woman to go on.

'I was losing my strength, Ellie. I lost the power to merge, and one day I realised I could be seen among the rocks. It was then that I decided you'd be safer if I sent you into the world.'

'Me?' I stared at her in bewilderment.

Nanny came over and brushed my forehead with her beard. 'You were the child, Ellie.' She turned back to the old woman.

'I hailed some passing herders and asked them to take you to the home of Alma West. She was the one I'd cured and I knew where she lived. I doubted she'd still be alive – time flows quickly there – but I knew she'd have descendants.'

My head was spinning. So this lady was the same Ilk who'd saved Pop's great grandmother. And the goat girl from Nanny's story was Ilk's daughter, and what was she saying about a baby? It was hard to understand. Bits of information flowed past me like sticks on a flooded river.

'I paid the herders to take you,' Ilk said.

Nanny picked up one of my plaits in her mouth and gave it a gentle tug.

'I went too,' she murmured. 'Because you were still tiny and needed to be fed. Then Ilk was on her own.'

'What are you saying?' I cried.

The old woman came to me and took my hand. 'You're Gola's daughter. And you're my granddaughter,' she said.

'I'm the daughter of the goat girl?' It was almost too much to take in.

I lay back and stared at the roof of the cave. Stories were colliding in my mind – Oma's story about Alma West, Nanny's story of the goat girl. The tales crossed over and two worlds met: my home at Spit Farm and the world of the Gleam country beyond the Palisades. It put me in mind of the map I'd drawn in the sand tray at Stolt, where one path crossed the other and I'd marked the spot with stars. But here the crossing points weren't stars; they were people, and I was one of them.

'You're a child of the Gleam land.' Ilk closed both hands over mine and continued talking urgently. 'After you and Nanny left I was on my own, except for Harland. He was here. He still is.' She ran her fingers through her hair.

'There were times when he heard the instrument playing in the world and would have gone after it. I managed to hold him back. But then I grew weak and maybe he grew clever, because he'd try and send his seeming; that was harder to hold.'

'What do you mean?' I asked.

'His seeming,' she said. 'His likeness. It has his looks but it's just an appearance. It's not really there.' Ilk shook her head and spoke quietly. 'The day came when I found Harland trying to leave the Gleam country and it took the last of my strength to keep him here; his body, that is – I couldn't hold his likeness. It travelled free as a bird. He hadn't tried to leave for ages. I don't know what prompted it.'

'It was me,' I said. 'The button-box was in pieces and I was the one who put it back together.'

We were quiet for a long time after that. Ilk looked exhausted by what she'd told me, and I was numb with shock. She went back to the fire and squatted beside the pot, checking the curd by lamplight.

I tried to make sense of it all.

'So Harland was using Luca. He needed someone to carry the button-box.'

'He'd rather it had been you,' Ilk said. 'Then he would have got everything he wanted.'

I sat up with a jolt. If Harland — the real Harland and not the seeming — got his hands on the button-box there'd be no hope for Oma! And what of Luca? Poor Luca. He'd come on this journey to help me and where was he now? Was he out there under the sky or was he still in the tunnels? I had to try to reach him.

Ilk tasted the curd again. 'It will be ready by morning. Now we wait.'

'I can't wait,' I cried. 'I've got to find Luca.'

'Too late. He's with Harland.' She looked up in surprise. 'It's working,' she cried. 'It's not set but it's already working! I can see the boy clearly and I know where he is.'

She took a spoonful of the curd and closed her eyes. When she opened them I noticed a change in her. Her back straightened and she grew calm and steady. She filled a bowl and handed it to me.

'They're on Shine Mountain,' she said. 'Harland's in the hut where you were born. And right now he's repairing the button-box. He's replacing the lost reeds and other parts of that cursed instrument. When he plays it next he wants to hear the sound. You must leave the Gleam land immediately, for your safety.'

I didn't respond to her words, but took a mouthful of curd. It was fresh and sweet. It tasted a bit like the curd Oma made, but it wasn't the same. As it slipped down my throat I felt my energy returning. I seemed to grow, in strength and in courage. The feeling spread from my belly to the tips of my fingers and I thought of Dr Elixir's Original Extract. But Stumpy's medicine was fake, and this was real. In a few minutes I felt completely different. It was as if I hadn't been travelling for weeks, as if I'd never caused a drought, as if nothing bad could ever happen again. I put my hands to my face. My chapped lips were better and my windburnt skin was smooth.

I watched Ilk. She stood up and went to Sol, and although she was old I saw she was no longer frail. She took my milking mug from the saddlebag and filled it with curd, stretching a piece of oilcloth over the top and tying it with string. 'For your grandmother,' she said. 'If you're quick it will heal her. Don't spill a drop. Galita will take you back.'

'What about you, Ilk?' Nanny asked.

'I can hold him now. I'm sure I can. I have gained the strength of many years. Take the underways, Galita. Go south when you reach the steeps.'

She handed me the mug and although she was smiling, her eyes looked sad. 'It's been wonderful to see you, Ellie. You have your mother's face and something of her spirit. Now mount your horse and go home.'

I faced her, looking steadily into her eyes. 'I'm not leaving,' I told her. 'I haven't done what I came to do. And I would never leave without Luca.'

Ilk stared at me in alarm. 'You don't understand, Ellie. You have no choice. This is your one chance. If you hear that music you won't be *able* to leave.'

It was getting light outside. I could see a wooden gate at the far end of the cave.

'Go now,' Ilk said, pointing in the opposite direction.

I looked towards the gate. 'What happens if I go this way?'

'You'll come out in the dead land at the base of the mountain,' Ilk said. 'If you go that way, you'll be playing into his hands.'

When I climbed on Sol, Ilk reached up and grabbed my wrist. 'Go to your oma. Ellie, please. It's too danger-ous. I'll do what I can for your friend.'

'That might not be enough!'

Nanny bleated in panic as I turned Sol towards the gate and urged him into a canter. He cleared the gate easily in one smooth leap, his hoofs sending out a shower of sparks when he landed.

'No, Ellie – don't!' I heard Ilk cry. I took no notice.

28

Shine Mountain

IF I THOUGHT I'd seen ruined country before, it was nothing compared with the Gleam land. It wasn't a place of sweet grass and endless streams. There was no corn so tall you had to fell it with an axe. Nothing grew. No blade of grass, not one stunted tree. The sun shone on bare rock, and the glare was intense. After the cool of the underways I felt I'd entered a furnace.

Shine Mountain towered above me, and the trail I was on weaved across the lower slopes before heading straight up, disappearing into a field of boulders.

A hot wind blew in my face and burnt the insides of my nostrils. I held my shirt over my nose so I could breathe, and leaned forward as Sol raced up the trail. As we climbed, the stones gave off a white heat and the way ahead began to shimmer. I closed my eyes and listened to Sol's hoofs clattering on the stone. When I opened them I saw a fork in the track, one way veering around the side of the mountain, the other heading straight ahead.

I let Sol choose, and he took the steep path. It narrowed and grew more dangerous with each stride. He slowed to a walk and scrambled up the incline, picking his way through loose stones that rolled out from under his hoofs. When we reached a place where the path was blocked by a rockfall, I slipped to the ground and unbuckled the waterbag. I took the curd from my saddlebag and poured some in the water. I figured that if I ran out of strength it would help me with the climb.

'Wait here, Sol. If I'm not back by night, go home.'

He gazed into my eyes and put his nose to mine. I kissed him goodbye and climbed over the rock pile.

The path beyond was made of small white pebbles, just like the ones in Auntie Lil's necklace. Whoever said they were lucky? If it hadn't been for those stones I wouldn't have paid the tinker and the button-box would have stayed in pieces. I wouldn't be here. Oma would be well and Luca would be safe and sound, doing rope tricks with the medicine show. I stopped to catch my breath and picked one up.

'Ouch!' The pebble was so hot it stuck to my fingers. I dropped it immediately.

At home I used to walk for days over Mt Ossa. I knew every part of it, from the south face to Blade Ridge to the Saddle and the Hazards beyond. My balance was good and my legs were strong, and even with my bad foot I had climbed the summit more times than I could count. I knew nothing of this mountain, but I felt the path was leading me in the right direction. Despite the heat and blinding glare, I quickly gained height.

In the distance was a sheer rock wall, which seemed impassable. But when I came close I found a cleft in the face that was just my size. I wedged myself into it and looked up. Far above, the crack narrowed slightly, but there was no shortage of holds. I reached up and found a purchase above my head. Then, jamming my foot in the crack, I began climbing, using my elbows and knees to inch skywards.

I don't think Luca could have come this way, unless the button-box had dragged him straight up the crevice.

By the time I reached the top, the wind had dropped. I looked back and saw the vast dead land below. There was no sound and no sign of life; nothing moved.

I drank from the waterbag, then continued, crossing a plateau studded with giant rocks that had fallen from above. There was a tiny lake ahead. The water was the colour of snowmelt, a milky green, and the summit reared above it. A figure was silhouetted against the sky up there, someone on their hands and knees. I heard the sound of a hammer hitting stone. Clink, clink, clink.

Moving from one boulder to the next, I made my way to the lake, hoping I wouldn't be seen.

An old wooden hut stood overlooking the water. *This must be it*, I thought, *Ilk's hut!* The door was open and I could hear someone humming. It was the same tune I'd heard in the way-wagon at the Trading Post.

I skirted the lake and approached the hut from the side, keeping out of sight. When I peered through the boards I saw Harland leaning over a bench. I knew it was the real Harland and not his likeness, because he held a screwdriver in one hand and the button-box in the other. He had the end plate off and he was peering inside the bellows. His humming resonated in the soundbox. I was very close to him, even closer than I'd been in the way-wagon. I held my breath and my skin prickled. He was intent on his work and didn't notice me. Parts of the instrument were spread out on the table, and when he glanced up I saw that his left eye was no different from his right; both eyes were cold and grey and there was no sign of that swirling cloud.

Luca wasn't in the hut so I guessed it was him I'd seen on the rocks above. I slipped behind the building and climbed a set of rough stone steps that led to a great pillar of rock that had a door at its base. When I went inside I found the steps continued, spiralling upwards like the stairs inside a tower – only this tower hadn't been built of stone, it had been hollowed out of the mountain. I heard the hammering again. It echoed down the stairwell.

I put the waterbag over my shoulder and began climbing. The steps weren't wide and I had to hug the wall. Up I went, higher and higher. I was panting hard by the time I saw sky above. I expected the stairs would come out on top of the mountain but they didn't. They narrowed to a manhole and when I crawled through it I saw I'd arrived at the base of the summit rock. Luca was ahead, working with his back to me. He had a mallet in one hand and a chisel in the other and he was cutting steps out of the bare rock, leading to the top. He still had his rope slung over his chest. He worked like one possessed, splitting off great chunks of stone, which then slid away, clattering down the mountain. It was hot up there but his face was deathly pale. He looked exhausted. More than exhausted – he looked barely alive.

'Luca, stop!'

If he heard, he gave no sign. He finished one step and moved to the next, striking blow after blow.

'Luca,' I cried. 'It's me, Ellie.'

I ran to him and tried to grab the mallet, but I couldn't stay his hand. The power behind the blow was such that my weight made no difference. Bang! The mallet struck the chisel and another chunk of stone broke free. I stood behind him and put both my arms around him, trying to stop him working the way I'd tried to stop the button-box. I might not have even been there. He continued striking the rock with frightening strength, and I realised he must have cut the steps I'd just climbed.

'Luca, please stop. You're killing yourself.'

He took no notice. Sweat ran into his eyes and his breath rasped in his chest. I wondered when he'd last drunk and suddenly I remembered the waterbag. I unscrewed the lid and held the bag to his lips. He didn't drink. He didn't even notice it was there. The water ran out the sides of his mouth and trickled down his chin. But he must have swallowed a few drops, because he began to falter. The chisel slipped out of his hand and he slowly lowered the mallet. He stared at it as if he didn't know what it was.

'More, Luca,' I cried, lifting the waterbag. 'Drink.'

He swallowed a mouthful and turned to me with a dazed look. Then he grabbed the bag with both hands and gulped. He didn't stop until he'd drained the very last drop. When he handed it back I could see he'd come to his senses.

'Ellie—'

'Don't talk, Luca. You're all right. We have to get away from here. We have to—'

Luca looked over my shoulder and his eyes grew wide. I heard a footstep.

'What? Not finished yet?' I swung around and saw Harland emerging from the manhole. He had the button-box over his shoulder. 'Useless boy! I've finished my work but you haven't finished yours.'

Luca flinched as if he'd been hit.

'I should hurl you over the edge.' Harland gestured beyond the steps to where the rock fell away into nothing. 'But I won't,' he said, 'because today is a perfect day and nothing can spoil it.'

He looked at me and smiled. 'I was going to play to bring you, my girl, but now I see there's no need. Instead I will play to celebrate your return.'

He put one hand on the button-box. 'I've repaired it. Soon you'll hear the sweetest music in the world. It will be heard all over the country.'

I looked around me, hoping there was somewhere to

hide. I wished I was like the goat girl and could merge with whatever was nearby. I wished I could disappear into the rocks and sky.

Luca had carved a dozen steps into the summit rock. Where the steps ended, the rockface was vertical. It wasn't impossibly high. If Luca helped me, I knew I could reach the top. I hoped there might be a way down the other side.

'Give me a leg up!' I nodded towards the rock.

'That's my girl,' Harland said. 'Go to the top. That's what I planned.' He stroked the instrument and sighed. 'I've waited so long for this day.'

Luca hoisted me up and Harland didn't attempt to stop him. I leaned down and took Luca's rope then I hauled while he scrambled up, using whatever tiny footholds he could find.

The summit wasn't more than ten paces across and it fell away steeply. We were very high and I felt dizzy looking down.

'We're trapped!' Luca cried.

My heart was thumping in my chest but I tried to still my mind and think.

'Harland can't make it up here without help,' I said. 'Have a close look around the side. If there's a ledge we could use the rope to get down.'

Luca lay on his stomach and looked over the edge. The drop was sheer and there was nothing to fix the rope to. He looked about in despair. 'It's no use, Ellie.'

I heard Harland laugh. 'Don't leave without me,' he called.

Then came the sound of the button-box. It wasn't wheezing or clacking; instead it played a run of perfect notes. A second later Harland's head and shoulders appeared, then he jumped to his feet and stood before us. 'I played a scale and climbed it like a ladder,' he said, pleased with himself. He spread his hands. 'Welcome to my land!'

I was fixed to the spot with fear but Luca stood up. He swung his lariat and the rope made a sound like roaring wind. When he took aim, Harland laughed and stepped aside, catching the rope with one hand. He pulled Luca towards him, then flung the boy aside with a force that would have carried him over the edge if I hadn't grabbed him.

'Do your weather, Luca!' I cried. 'Do it now!'

Luca looked at me, terrified.

'Call in the skies like Pappy Storm did! Like this—' I let go of him and banged my fists together. He stared, not understanding.

'Do it!' I cried. 'Copy me.'

Hesitantly, he put one fist on top of the other and when he did this I heard rumbling in the distance. He looked up, his eyes wide with surprise and confusion.

'Good, Luca!' I cried. I raised my hand and pointed to the sky, then I made the same circling motion I'd seen in the dream. 'Now stir the winds!'

Luca followed and the sky responded with a gust that lifted his hair and blew up the collar of Harland's frockcoat.

'That's it!' I said.

Harland barely noticed. He was staring at me the
way a range-cat stares at a rabbit, and when I met his
eyes I froze. He lifted the button-box and seemed about
to play – but then he sighed and lowered it.

'I always knew this moment would come,' he said.
'My daughter and I standing on top of the world, the
future stretched before us.'

His words knocked the breath out of me. Had
I heard him right?

My daughter?

'You don't know?' he asked, taking a step towards
me. 'You don't know who you are?'

He paused and shook his head. 'You're my child,
mine and Gola's. The proof of our love.'

My heart thudded in my chest and for several
seconds I could hear nothing but the roaring in my ears.
I wanted to scream that it couldn't be true. But I wasn't
sure. I closed my eyes and thought I might be sick,
but I swallowed it down. When I opened my eyes the
mountain was spinning around me. I took a deep breath
and tried to hold still, tried to stop the earth moving
under my feet. I was Gola's daughter – that much was
true. Ilk had said I was Gabe's child. Gabe was the one
Gola had wanted to name on her promise day. Gabe
was the one she had pined for. But here was Harland
standing in front of me, claiming me for his own.

'We have much to look forward to,' he said, taking
another step towards me.

I backed away, glancing at Luca. I didn't think he'd
heard what Harland had said. He was staring at the

sky. The wind dropped. I watched him lick his finger and hold it up, testing the air. Then, hesitantly, he made the circling motion again. When the wind returned he looked amazed.

'I can see it now, my girl – you and I, working together.' Harland gazed at me and then at the instrument. 'We'll build a mansion on the mountain and live like royalty. With the help of the button-box there'll be no end to what we'll achieve.'

I looked again at Luca. I had to give him time. I was thinking fast.

'You...you're my father?' I said, my voice full of fear and uncertainty.

'Yes, my dear, and I have been waiting so long for you to come home to me.'

'Home? I don't have a home.'

'Oh but you will, my darling girl. It should have been the three of us all this time – me, you and your mother. But your mother ran from my love so we never had the life we should have lived. But now that you are here, we'll build a home and live together, just as we were meant to – as a family.'

The word 'family' brought Oma to my mind – Oma, who had brought me up and cared for me all my life. And now, looking at this man – maybe my father, my blood, maybe not – I knew with more certainty than I'd ever felt about anything, that Oma, Pop, Tod and the aunties were my real family, and always would be, no matter what. That knowledge brought a surge of strength every bit as powerful as the curd, and I let it flow into my performance. Because that's what it was. I made myself appear desperate and bewildered, even though for the first time since I left home – since before Pop died – I didn't feel confused at all.

'I – I knew I never belonged with those people on Spit Farm,' I began. 'I travelled so far...to find my family, my real family.'

'And now you've found me.' Harland opened his arms, stretching the bellows of the button-box. It didn't groan; it made a rich chord and I felt it tug me forward.

I looked to Luca. He was still watching the sky. The perfect blue had become streaked with grey and there were dark clouds in the west. His eyes met mine and I saw a change in him. It was as if he was remembering something long forgotten. He gazed at his hands and then looked up and stirred the sky. The wind blew off my hat and rolled it across the ground. It grew so strong that it spun Luca around.

Harland tucked the button-box under his arm and held out his hand to me.

'Welcome home, my child.'

At that moment Luca dug in his heels and came to a halt. The wind dropped and the air grew still. The sun was gone and the day was suddenly dark. He stood tall and a wall of clouds quietly massed behind him.

'Drop it,' Luca said, pointing to the instrument.

Harland threw back his head and laughed. He thought the boy was joking. But Luca was deadly serious. Luca put his palms together and stared at the ground. Then he repeated his request. His voice was quiet, but the clouds were banking all around. Harland noticed them.

'It's mine!' Harland said, holding the button-box close. He seemed uncertain for a second and that's when Luca reached for the sky. The air crackled around him and his hair began to rise. I threw myself to the ground.

'Be careful, Luca!' I cried.

There was a flash off to the south and Harland jumped back, looking across at the lightning. It forked and branched like the fine bright roots of some plant that lives and dies in an instant. He grasped the button-box to his chest and for a moment he was frightened. He seemed like some hunted thing, holding the instrument as if his life depended on it. I could see the want in him. He wanted power, he wanted the button-box and, more than anything, he wanted me. Then the lightning moved off to the north and he recovered his composure. He held out his hand again.

'Come, my daughter. What a life we will lead.'

I had to trust that Luca knew what he was doing. Very carefully I stood up. I went and picked up my hat and when I'd put it back on I faced Harland. 'I want that life,' I said. 'I want a family. But how can I trust you? How do I know that you won't hurt me like you hurt my mother?'

'You think I didn't love your mother? You think I won't love you? You are MINE, girl. You are meant to be with me. Forever and ever – I will never let you go.'

'I think you only want that button-box,' I said quietly.

Harland looked shocked. He did up the catch on the instrument then placed it on his open palm. 'I made this for Gola. It was a gift of love.' He gazed at the button-box with admiration. 'It's the finest thing I've ever made.'

He took off his hat and gave a low bow.

'Let me prove my love,' he said. 'What's mine is yours.'

He stretched out his arm, offering me the instrument.

'You don't believe me?' he cried, when I didn't move towards him. 'It's yours. Here, have it!'

He tossed the instrument in my direction, and the instant he did, Luca put his palms together and made the lightning sign. Luca's hair stood on end, reaching for the lightning but just before it struck he flexed his wrist and showed the flat of his hand, swiping the bolt aside so that it hit the button-box instead of him.

The mountain flared in blinding light and time slowed down. The little instrument seemed to hang in the air. Then the catch burst open and the bellows stretched and twisted, making a honking cry that ended with a hiss. The air was full of an acrid scent which made me think of burning hair. Perhaps it was the smell of Harland's rage.

Luca made the sign again and a second strike followed the first. The tin grille of the button-box sparked and then glowed cherry red. Harland looked small and shocked and for a moment I thought that he'd been hit. When the third bolt reached its mark the button-box exploded with a flash.

I covered my eyes with my hands and saw Harland's

bright shadow on the inside of my eyelids. He was grasping towards me and clenching his fists, his face twisted in fury. Slowly the image faded. I rubbed my eyes and when I looked again I saw an old man stooping in the wind.

I blinked and stared. Harland's thick hair had grown thin and his frockcoat flapped around him. His skin had become crumpled paper. He looked like the ghost of himself, ancient and frail, as if the loss of the instrument was more than he could bear.

Luca lowered his hands, and although the sky remained full of heavy clouds, the lightning moved off, sheets of blue flashing away into the distance. He took my hand and we both stared at Harland, at what he was becoming. He continued to change – shrivelling and shrinking, and soon he was smaller than a child. Then he was no bigger than a cat – not a range-cat, but a barn cat. Then he was the size of a rat, and I could see he was no longer living. He was the remains of something that had once lived, long ago; mummified remains, a bit of hide and cloth and hair. Then that dried up and crumbled. All that was left was a small pile of dust, which blew away in the wind.

29

The Way Home

LUCA AND I STOOD staring at the place where Harland had been. There was nothing left of the button-box except a faint smell of burning. Luca let go of my hand and looked across the country. The lightning was far away to the south now, but the storm had not passed. The clouds overhead were so heavy I could almost feel the weight of them.

'Don't stop, Luca.' I flicked my fingers the way Pappy Storm had done. Luca blinked and shook his head.

'Not like that. That's for a shower.'

He frowned and cupped his hands, then he raised them to the sky as if he was offering something. There was an almighty clap of thunder.

The skies opened and the rain poured down.

All sorts of weather passed across Luca's face — storms and sunshine, clouds and rain. He stared at his open hands as if he couldn't believe it.

'You did it!' I cried. 'You're a weatherman!'

Luca was laughing and crying at the same time. He danced in the downpour, shouting and whooping above the noise. I joined him, splashing in the puddles that were quickly forming at our feet. We were soaked to the skin. Water pooled in the brim of my hat and when I dipped my head it cascaded onto the rock. I opened my arms to the sky, and my mouth as well. Then I stared at the clouds.

'Send them east!' I cried, pointing.

Luca brushed one hand over the other. He made a winding motion and I watched the clouds roll overhead. The rain didn't let up. I took off my hat and raised my face to the sky so I could feel it on my eyelids. It pelted down and I imagined thousands of tiny streams flowing down the mountain into the land below. I could hear them in my mind – trickling, bubbling, gushing – and, above the sound, I heard a high-pitched cry.

I opened my eyes and looked down off the summit. Nanny Gitto stood on the steps below. She called out something and stamped her foot.

'What?' I yelled, lurching towards her, laughing.

'I'm too old for this sort of climbing,' she cried. 'Stop that fooling!'

Even though the drought had broken, Nanny did not look happy. 'Ilk says you have to come at once. If the tunnels flood you won't get back in time.'

'In time for what?' I asked, and then all at once I stopped laughing because I knew – *in time for Oma*. I tossed Luca his rope.

'Let's go!'

Luca lowered me to the steps then jumped down after me.

～～

THE JOURNEY DOWN Shine Mountain was much faster than the way up. When we reached the bottom of the stairs, I would have liked to stop and see the hut where I was born. I could have stood at the window and gazed out over the lake. It didn't look so little now. But there was no time to linger and wonder about the life I could have led, or to listen out for sounds from the distant past: my mother, Gola, calling to her herd, *Yidda yidda yidda!* Sounds from the present filled my ears – a cricket chirping, a frog croaking and the wheeling cry of a rainbird somewhere overhead. The land was coming back to life.

We went on, and I realised that the stone path I'd followed coming up was actually a dry creek bed. It was already flowing fast, the water rushing over the white pebbles.

Nanny told us to hold her horns. The stones were slippery and with one of us on either side she ran beside the creek, skittering over the ground and dragging us with her. She paused when we reached the rockfall, tossing her head and shaking her tail. I had forgotten how she hated to be wet. Raindrops collected on her eyelashes and dripped down her face. She let out a mournful cry and I knew it wasn't just the rain that was upsetting her.

'Nanny, what's wrong?'

'Nothing,' she said. 'Collect some stones if you're going to.'

'What? Why?'

'Moonstones, Ellie. Haven't I taught you anything? Surely you're going to replace the ones you stole?'

I quickly filled my pockets then Nanny pulled us over the rock pile.

Sol nickered when we appeared, his eyes shining and his coat slick, washed clean of the dust that had covered him. Before long he was carrying us into the foothills, following Nanny as she ran along the trail.

Ilk was waiting at the entrance to the goat cave. Her hair was wet and rain dripped off her chin. She had the gate open and the doe from Slattern Creek was standing beside her.

She checked the milking mug in my saddlebag, then reached up and took my hand. She took Luca's as well. 'I don't know how to thank you. Without you two this country would have been lost. I was almost lost myself.'

'Harland's gone, Ilk, and so is—'

She waved my words away. 'I know,' she said. 'His rage was in the button-box. It was his life. It held him in the world.'

She put her hand on Sol's moon mark. 'Go well, shine mount,' she whispered, and to me she said, 'Farewell my child, I think you'll find your way.'

I suddenly felt sad about leaving Ilk so soon. She was the grandmother I'd never known and now there was no time.

'There'll be time later,' Nanny said. 'Goodbye, Ellie.'

I looked at her in bewilderment. 'What do you mean, goodbye?'

Nanny looked at Ilk then up at me.

'I'm not coming.'

'Of course you're coming. You're my goat. You're coming with me. You're Oma's goat as well.'

Nanny shook her head in irritation.

'Don't be silly, girl. I belong to myself and I belong here in the Gleam country. You're grown now and must stand on your own two feet. You must look to the future and so must I.'

I slipped off Sol and held her face in my hands, staring into her golden eyes.

'Nanny, you're coming!'

'What have I told you about being bossy? I'm needed here. Ilk and I are starting a new herd.'

'It will be as it once was,' Ilk said. 'A magnificent herd. And the country too will flourish again.'

Just then I heard the sound of bleating and the two kids appeared, running over the bank at the side of the goat cave, their mouths full of chickweed and their knees stained green.

'It's happening already,' Ilk said.

Nanny gave me a gentle nudge and her voice was soft. 'Go quickly, Ellie.'

'But Nanny—' I felt tears well up.

'No buts. You do your job and I'll do mine. You're not a child now. You're a grown way-girl and soon you'll be a way-woman.'

'You can visit,' Ilk said. 'It's not far by the underways.'

'Yes,' I whispered, stifling a sob.

Nanny put her cheek to mine, first on one side and then the other. 'Farewell, Ellie. Make your grandma proud of you. Make both your grandmothers proud.'

Ilk put her arms around both of us, then she stood back and adjusted my shawl.

'I made this for you when you were tiny.' She kissed me on the forehead. 'Go now and travel well.'

Sol snorted and pawed the ground, impatient to be on his way. Luca leaned forward and helped me back into the saddle. I looked down at Ilk.

'That curd hasn't fixed my foot,' I said.

'Would you want it to?' she asked.

'Of course. What good has it ever done me?' As soon as I asked that question I remembered how my foot had saved me on the slope below Jutt Rock.

'And it may save you again,' Ilk said. 'Go well, my dear.'

I had no idea what she meant and there was no time to ask. Sol took off, cantering towards the passage at the rear of the cave. I turned and waved and my shawl flowed out behind me.

THE TUNNEL ROOF was bright with stars. Glowworms, I thought. Or fireflies. I hadn't noticed them before. As we travelled on I sent my mind above and imagined life returning, the vast brown plains greening as we passed.

We weaved our way downhill through branching passages and found the pool where we had stopped to drink. Was it only yesterday? The pool had broken its banks and there was no sound of dripping water. Instead I heard a torrent raging somewhere nearby. The roar of it echoed through the cavern.

Sol galloped on, and when we met a river he plunged straight in. We clung to his mane as he swam across. I hoped the curd was safe in the saddlebag – there was no time to check. Sol reached the other side and scrambled up the bank, racing onwards. The way grew steep and I had to clasp my hands around his neck to stop us sliding off over his tail.

I don't know how much time that journey took. Perhaps it was a day, or perhaps just one long evening. I let Sol choose our path, and he knew the way to go. The wind rushed past my ears and when Sol finally slowed to a trot, splashing through a creek, I realised the cold air of the tunnels had grown warm.

'Steam,' I said, sniffing the air. The smell of it reminded me of the washpool. A few minutes later we emerged from the shade-cave into the light.

*

IT WAS EVENING on Spit Farm. The place looked worse than when I had left. The hills were barren and the ground was bare – the rain had not reached here.

Deep cracks ran across the path that led to the wash-pool and Sol had to watch his footing. He slowed to a walk and my heart sank. The land felt old and tired. I doubted Oma could have survived.

Tod was the first person I saw. He was watering the goats, pouring half a bucket into the trough below the kitchen window.

'Ellie!' he yelled, his eyes wide with disbelief. 'Ellie, you came back!'

His face broke into a broad smile but then it clouded over.

'How could you leave like that? Oma almost died of worry.'

'Almost?' I cried.

Mooti and Gus appeared, Mooti barking and careering in circles while Gus sat at my feet, thumping his tail on the ground. The sound of the dogs brought Shirley Serpentine to the door of the shack.

'You again,' she said. 'I thought we'd seen the back of you! And who's this you've brought?'

'This is Luca. He's a rainmaker and weatherman.'

I grabbed the mug of curd out of the saddlebag and rushed past Shirl to the back room.

Oma was lying on our palliasse with her eyes half closed. I don't know what I expected but her appearance shocked me more than I can say. She was tiny and her skin was so thin I could see through it to the bones below. I knew she'd reached the end of her strength. She was barely alive and I wondered if she could still hear and see.

'Oh, Oma!' I gasped.

She opened her eyes at that; they began watering. Was it tears? She reached for me and tried to speak, but all that came out was a dry whisper. 'Shhh, Oma, take this,' I said, and I gave her a spoonful of curd. Her lips were cracked and the end of the spoon clinked against her teeth.

'Another,' I said. 'Open your mouth.'

I could see the effort it cost her. She licked her lips and swallowed.

'Oma, you're going to get better,' I told her. I watched her face anxiously, wishing it to be true. There was no change for several moments – if anything she seemed to grow paler. Then her eyes slid to one side and her eyelids closed, reminding me of the day Fat Hattie died.

'Oma, no!' I cried. I was too late.

She was very still. I grasped for her bony hand. And then, just as a sob was bursting from my chest, her eyelids flicked open. She looked at me and her eyes cleared.

'Ellie,' she said in a croaky voice. Her eyes seemed full of both happiness and sadness, but she didn't yet have the strength to say anything more than, 'Another.'

I gave her a third spoonful of curd and watched the change in her. It was like seeing somebody come back to life. Her parched skin grew softer and colour bloomed in her cheeks. She squeezed my hand.

'I'm sorry for lying to you, Ellie,' she whispered.

'Shhh, just rest, Oma,' I said. 'It's okay. I'm sorry for running away.'

She smiled and her face, with all its lines, was a map I could easily read. I saw pleasure and a future.

'Oma. I took the button-box back.'

'My brave girl,' she said.

Just then I heard voices in the kitchen.

'She's back! Thank goodness.'

Auntie Lil came in the door, followed by Uncle Vern.

'Ellie, it's so good to—' My uncle stopped mid-sentence. He gaped at Oma and Auntie Lil did too.

'Flo, how...?'

Oma raised her hand. She took another spoonful of the curd. 'Our girl,' she muttered.

After a few more mouthfuls she sat up. Lil and Vern looked at her in astonishment.

'You're coming good, Flo!' Auntie Lil clasped her hands to her chest.

Oma nodded and looked around

'Where's Tod?' she asked.

I told her he was outside with Sol.

'And Nanny Gitto? Did you put her in the barn?'

'She stayed, Oma. She stayed in the Gleam land. She came from there.'

There was a lot to explain, so much that I didn't know where to begin. I was wondering how to start when I heard Tod and Luca come into the kitchen. Oma heard them too.

'We have a visitor,' she said. 'Lil, Vern, go and make him welcome.'

After they had left Oma leaned towards me. She ran

her fingers through my hair. 'You've changed,' she said. 'You're no bigger, but you've grown somehow.'

'I'm a way-girl,' I told her. 'Or I'm becoming one. I can make maps and sometimes I can see a little way ahead.'

'What do you see now?' she asked.

'Rain. It's coming from the west.' I opened the window and let in a cool draught of air. 'But you can see that for yourself.'

Oma looked out. The sky was low and overcast.

'It's true,' she cried. 'You're bringing the rain with you.'

'Not me. It's my friend who brings the rain. His name is Luca. He can change the weather.'

As I spoke I heard the first splattering of raindrops on the roof. They grew steadier, heavier, and soon there was a downpour. My grandmother sank back on her pillows and closed her eyes with a deep sigh. 'There's no better sound,' she said.

'Oma, there's so much to tell you.'

Oma gave a yawn and smiled. 'Just listen to that rain.'

She shook her head as if she couldn't believe it. Then she yawned again.

'I want to hear everything, Ellie,' she murmured, already drifting off. 'I'll see you in the morning. And we can start from the beginning.'

30

Mud Map

LUCA LEFT EARLY the next day. We lent him one of
the ponies and I went with him as far as Jutt Rock. The
air was fresh and cool after the rain and I could hear
the creeks flowing as they made their way to Spit River.
I walked with my hand on the pony's wither. Luca's
long legs trailed the ground.

'Take the south road over the pass,' I said. 'There's a
way-hut near the ridge and once you reach the turn-off
you'll be heading to the Trading Post. From there you'll
find your way. Can you thank Rye for the wishbone?
Tell him it worked a charm. And give these to Meridian.'
I handed him three moonstones. 'For the past, present
and future,' I said.

Luca put them in his pocket. When we reached Jutt
Rock he stepped off the pony and stood looking across
the valley. He scraped some mud from his boot and

studied the ground. 'I wish I had something to give you, Ellie. A present to say goodbye.'

'You broke the drought. That's enough.'

He squatted for a moment, closing his eyes. Then he opened one hand and made a long slow arc that went from east to west. 'For the future, Ellie. For your future.'

He stood up and watched the sky. When nothing happened, he grinned and shrugged. 'That one might need practice,' he said.

I took his hand. 'Our paths will cross again, Luca. It could be sooner than you think. Tell Meridian I'm coming.'

'How will you know where we are?'

'I'll know.'

We hugged goodbye, and Luca mounted the pony and rode on. I watched him all the way to Bald Hill. He paused when he reached the top and looked back. Then he made the sign again. It was really just a wave. I waved in return and we went our separate ways, him towards the pass and me to the clearing above Jutt Rock.

There were pine needles and leaf litter on Pop's grave. I swept it clear and told him what I'd done.

'The button-box is gone, Pop. I took it back.'

As I spoke I looked up and saw mist rising from the valley. The faintest hint of a rainbow appeared above Bald Hill.

'I'm going to be a way-lady,' I said. 'I'm going to learn from Meridian. Sometimes I'll travel with the medicine show and sometimes I'll stay at home. And I'll visit the

Gleam land again. I need to check on Nanny Gitto and get to know my other grandma.'

I sat down against a tree and wondered if it was all true, if that really was what my future held.

A mud map, I thought, and I drew a circle on the wet ground. I threw Pop's hat into the ring and tried to let the map make itself.

'Who's it for?' I heard Meridian ask.

'It's for me.'

'Then follow your footsteps.'

I closed my eyes and saw my tracks: my odd footprints with one foot heading forward and the other heading back. They seemed to be going in circles, weaving in and out and crossing each other. They headed east, then spun to the west. I realised they were dancing. Two steps forward and two steps back. Heel, toe and around we go. The steps were uneven but the rhythm was true, and I could see a pattern forming. When I looked closer I noticed the print on the soles had changed.

'They're pretty,' Meridian said. 'Such fine stitching. And you can always see where you're going because the stones glow in the dark.'

A pair of boots shone in my mind. They were midnight blue and the sides were studded with moonstones. They were strong and comfortable, good for walking and good for dancing, too. And there was dancing to be done. I could feel it in my bones.

I opened my eyes and looked around the clearing. It was full of dappled sunlight. Rain dripped from the trees and a little lake had formed in the crown of Pop's hat. The rainbow was brighter now. It stretched from Bald Hill all the way across the valley. I couldn't see where it ended.

I smoothed the ground in front of me, ready to begin.

ABOUT THE AUTHOR

JULIE HUNT loves poetry, storytelling and traditional folktales. Her debut novel *Song for a Scarlet Runner* won the inaugural Readings Children's Book Prize and her graphic novel *KidGlovz* (illustrated by Dale Newman) won the 2016 Queensland Literary Award. She also writes books for younger readers. Her picture book, *The Coat* (illustrated by Ron Books), won the 2013 CBCA Picture Book of the Year. She lives on a farm in southern Tasmania and works in a library.

ALSO BY JULIE HUNT

'A gripping tale... I raced through it
feeling like an explorer on the edge of discovery.'
ANNA FIENBERG

Julie Hunt
SONG FOR A
SCARLET
RUNNER